YELLOW HORSE

A SAGE COUNTRY NOVEL

By Dan Arnold

YELLOW HORSE

This is a work of fiction. Names, places, characters and incidents are a work of the author's imagination or are used fictionally. Any resemblance or reference to any actual locales, events or persons, living or dead is entirely fictional.

Cover design by Dan Arnold

Photo credit © Dan Arnold

Fiction

Thrillers

Other Books by Dan Arnold/Daniel Roland Banks

Fiction

Archeological Thrillers

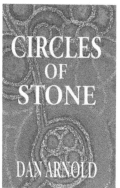

Other Books by Dan Arnold/Daniel Roland Banks

Fiction

Westerns

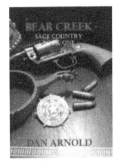
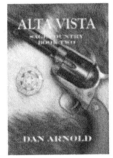

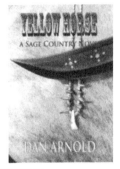

NON-FICTION

website: **www.danielbanks-books.com**

DAN ARNOLD

CHAPTER 1

Squatting to get a better look, the Comanche scout examined the ground. Looking back over his shoulder, he said, "The sign is clear, John, this trail is cold. Dutch Henry, his gang, and the mules he stole from the Army are well on their way to Colorado. When the storm hits we'll lose the trail altogether."

Texas Ranger Sergeant John Everett Sage swore, and said, "There're six of us on five horses. One man wounded. I don't see us catching up with him, do you?"

"No."

"If this don't beat all. We've been snake bit since we started. Three days in pursuit, one man wounded, and we lost two horses. I reckon it's time to turn back. The Army can chase Dutch Henry Bourne if they want to."

"If we're turning back, I'd like to ride over to Fort Sill. I want to visit my people."

"OK, we're going back to Eagle Springs to get Murphy patched up, and arrange for a couple of remounts. You can head on to Fort Sill and the Indian Territory from there. When you get there, tell the Army we lost Dutch Henry, and say hello to Quanah Parker for me."

Yellow Horse nodded in reply.

Sage said, "I figure I'll drift down to Spanish Fort. I hear Warren Crawford was last seen at Red River Station. I plan to take him, if I can."

"You want help?"

"Thanks, but I have these boys with me. If he's there I'll take a run at him.

Either way, when we get done there, we're expected at Fort Griffin. That's the wrong direction for you to be riding. When you get your business finished on the reservation you can catch up with us wherever we are"

Yellow Horse nodded again.

"…Could take some time."

Sage shrugged.

"Ain't scared. You'll find us."

Yellow Horse smiled.

"I always do."

Sage smiled back.

"I know. I just said that."

***

As the riders approached the middle of town, the tinny sound of the piano music being pounded out in the Lady Slipper Saloon was almost drowned out by the booming thunder and hammering rainfall.

At this time of year storms were to be expected, but this was a deluge. Turgid rainwater ran down the single street of Eagle Springs like a muddy river.

John Everett Sage and his bedraggled party of Texas Rangers sloshed to a stop in front of the livery stable, only to find the doors closed and no sign of life anywhere in sight. Even the pens beside the barn appeared to be empty.

Yellow Horse dismounted to open the barn door.

Coming in out of the storm was more than a relief. It was a complete change of existence; like being born again."

"Hap, Doc Johnson will be bending an elbow over in the saloon. Jim, go with him and see he gets patched up. We'll take care of the horses."

"OK, Cap'n , thanks."

"We'll meet you boys over there when you're done at the doc's, and don't call me Captain."

Ten minutes later, after struggling across the street through water high enough to overtop their boots, three Rangers and their scout walked into the Lady Slipper. They were all dripping water, and adding another layer to the trail of accumulated mud on the floor that began on the boardwalk just beyond the swinging doors.

Nobody in the saloon cared about any of that, as they'd all done the same thing. What caught the attention of the patrons was the presence of the dark skinned man with long braids, carrying a rifle in the crook of his arm. Seeing this, the piano player stopped beating noise out of the battered instrument.

Knowing things were about to get colorful, two of the Rangers selected seats at a table to watch what might happen next.

"Sage, is that fella an Injun?" The bartender asked.

John Sage looked at Yellow Horse with a wink.

"That's a good question. Is that right? Are you an Indian?"

Looking around the room, the scout said, "I am Yellow Horse. A warrior of the Comanche nation, a man of the Quahadi band."

Billy, the bartender pointed his finger at John Sage.

"You know we don't allow no Injuns in this establishment."

"You do now, Billy." Sage replied.

"Like hell I do. Boys, throw him out."

Several men started to stand, freezing in place when John Everett Sage cocked his pistol. He was holding it up near his shoulder, pointed at the ceiling.

"Sit down, gentlemen. There's no need for trouble, but if you want it, I'll meet you halfway."

Sage watched the men as they slowly sat back down.

"I don't care if you are the law, Sage. I don't have to serve no Injun."

"Shut up, Billy. No one asked you to serve him. It's pouring down rain and we've ridden more than thirty miles through it. I figure anyone has the right to come in out of the storm. If you say another word, I'll bust your head open."

The bartender didn't like it but he knew better than to press his luck.

Sage smiled and turned to the scout.

"Now then, brother, would you like a drink?"

The bartender started to protest, but John Sage slapped him across the side of the head with his pistol sending the man crashing to the floor.

Yellow Horse looked at Sage.

"No thanks, John. You know I don't drink the white man's fire water."

"Yep, I do. I just thought I'd be polite by makeing the offer."

Sage put his back to the bar and addressed the silent room, holstering his pistol.

"This man is James Yellow Horse. He's employed as a scout with Company D of the Texas Rangers, and he's been my friend for a good ten years. Anybody have any comments you'd care to pass."

Everyone in the room resumed doing what they'd been doing when the Rangers first walked in, with the exception of the bartender and the piano player. The former was still lying prone on the floor. The latter was swigging down a beer. When he finished, he wiped his lips on the back of his hand, and went back to torturing a tune from the reluctant keyboard.

The bartender staggered to his feet, gingerly touching the side of his head, where he found a tender welt, oozing a little blood.

He turned to find Sage staring at him with his head tilted to one side.

"My friend Yellow Horse and I will have coffee, Billy," Sage said, rapping his knuckles on the bar top.

The bartender stood there for a moment, swaying and blinking at him.

"Coffee?" He asked.

"Indeed, my good man. Step lively now."

"Yes sir, Mr. Sage, coffee coming right up."

The bartender stumbled away with his hand pressed to the side of his head.

Yellow Horse took off his hat and watched water drip from the brim.

"You didn't have to do that, John."

"People need to know I mean business. We're Texas Rangers. Respect is vital. If they think we're bluffing, they won't respect us."

"They'll never respect me."

"They will once they get to know you."

Yellow Horse wasn't so sure. Among his own people he was widely regarded as a valuable man. In his experience, white people seemed to have mixed opinions.

As Billy the bartender poured their coffee, Hap Wannamaker and Jim Gillett arrived in the somewhat wobbly company of Doc Johnson.

"You OK, Hap?" Sage asked.

"I reckon. The doc cleaned it out and sewed it up. Hurts like hell, though."

S'what choo get fer getting' shot." Doc Johnson mumbled.

Yellow Horse started laughing, and then the other Rangers joined in.

"What's so funny about that?" Doc Johnson asked.

"It's not you, Doc. It's Hap. He didn't *get* shot. He shot himself, got careless with his rifle." Yellow Horse said.

"Well, he ain't the first or the last to do that."

"That's not the funny part. He was sitting on his horse at the time. He was trying to put his rifle in the scabbard when it went off. The bullet went through his horse before it took a chunk out of him."

"That's not funny. How's the horse?"

With a frown, Hap said, "Dead, we had to put it down. Cap'n Sage was so mad; he threatened to do the same for me."

"…Which reminds me, Hap, I'm docking your pay for the remount—and stop calling me Captain."

The other Rangers were all chuckling.

"If you Rangers are through with the fun and games, you might apply your questionable skills to determining who killed everyone at the Morgan Settlement. As I was telling your friends here, somebody murdered um all, five men, three women and four children. They burned the whole place to the ground." Doc Johnson said.

"Indians?"

"Don't know, could be. Whoever did it, they made a bee line for the Indian Territory. What was the name of that Comanche? You know-- the one who jumped the reservation with his bunch, right after Christmas."

"You're thinking of Tu-ukumah. He didn't do it. All reports indicate he and his men are somewhere on the far side of the Llano Estacado. Were the horses shod?" Sage asked.

"Yep, the tracks was clear. They stole a wagon and a team, too."

"It wasn't any of my people. We don't have the equipment or the skills to keep our horses shod."

"Well, they stole everything they didn't burn. Probably have the equipment now."

"Whoever did it, the Indian Territory is federal. It's a matter for the army, or the U. S. Marshals. When did this happen?" Sage asked.

"Last night. Cowboy found the place smoldering this morning."

"No sign now." Yellow Horse said.

"No, this rain will have washed away their tracks." Sage agreed. "Doc, did you tell the army what happened?"

"Not yet. Several of us rode out to the settlement. We were burying the last of the bodies when the storm hit. We high tailed it back to town."

Sage looked at Yellow Horse, who nodded once in response.

"At first light, I'm going to the Territory. On the way, I'll have a look at the site. When I get to Fort Sill, I'll tell the army what happened and ask around. Maybe I'll learn something."

DAN ARNOLD

CHAPTER 2

The rocking and lurching of the stagecoach might've been acceptable if it weren't so violent and never ending. Since leaving Fort Worth, the country through which they traveled had become progressively more rocky, rough and broken.

Until this week, the ground had been much less uneven. It was as though the farther west one went, the worse the conditions became. The same would have to be said for the road. Could you even call this tortuous path a road?

A particularly sudden lurch threw Lucy Meadows almost into the ample lap of the woman seated beside her.

"Oh, I'm terribly sorry." Lucy said, as she tried to regain both her seat and her composure.

"Think nothing of it dearie. If you were packing a few more pounds you wouldn't bounce around so bad. Look at me. It would take an act of God to shake me out of my seat. When we get into the rough country, we may have to tie you down. Hah, hah, hah."

"When we get into the rough country? Why, I can't imagine it getting any worse than this."

The heavy set woman winked and held out her hand.

"Gertrude Andrews. This fellow to my left is my husband, Bucky."

"I'm pleased to meet you. My name is Lucy Meadows."

Lucy was aware the man who sat opposite her had been staring at her since they boarded the coach. His interest was not mere curiosity, but apparent lasciviousness.

The man seated next to him seemed disinterested in his traveling companions. His attention was generally fixed on the surrounding countryside. Unlike him, the man across from her was just plain leering at her. She'd never seen such open rudeness.

She had half a mind to tell him off, but another part of her brain told her to continue ignoring him.

"Where are you bound for, Miss Meadows?" Mrs. Andrews asked.

"…Fort Sill, in the Indian Territory. My father is stationed there. I haven't seen him for more than four years. He visited me in Maryland just before coming west. Please call me Lucy. Where are you folks headed?"

"…Home, to Spanish Fort, in Montague County."

"Goodness, is everything out here some kind of fort?"

The woman laughed again.

"No, dearie, but we've got plenty of um. This ain't exactly Boston or Saint Louis. We have marauding Indians, cutthroats and desperados by the bushel."

She scowled at Lucy's admirer. "It seems like all the riff raff drifted this way."

The unpleasant fellow worked his jaw like he was about to say something, but the man next to him turned toward him and said, "Mind your own business, friend. Put your eyes back in your head or I'll do it for you."

There was something in the way he said those words that left no question as to his sincerity.

Just then, the stage driver called out to the horses and the coach slowed to a halt. The driver hopped down and walked back to open the door of the coach.

"We gotta water the team at this creek. You ladies feel free to stretch your...What I mean is, you can walk around some if you feel the need. Don't wander far. Everything in this country will stick you, sting you, or stab you, and there's a buzz worm under every other bush."

Lucy looked at Mrs. Andrews.

"What's a buzz-worm?" She whispered.

"Hah, hah, hah. Honey, buzz worm is just the local name for rattle snakes. You usually won't see none, this time of year. This early in the spring it's still too cold. They won't crawl out of their dens till the ground warms up, maybe in a month or so. You stay with me and you'll be fine."

Lucy had considered finding a private spot somewhere, but she changed her mind.

"How far is it to the next rest stop?" she asked the driver.

"Next stop is Wichita Falls. That's about fifteen miles as the crow flies, but we ain't no crows. We'll be there in three or four hours. Now, you men give me a hand with the horses. The sooner we get this done, the sooner we'll be back under way."

CHAPTER 3

Yellow Horse approached the edge of the river with caution. Although he'd crossed here many times in the past, crossing after the violent spring thunderstorms when the water was highest, offered no small risk.

He sat for a moment listening to the churning and rushing of the usually slow moving, muddy water. It was even more red than usual and seemed almost to be a living thing. How often had he camped beside rivers and creeks like this, listening to the song of the waters? Today, it was not a song this river sang; it was more like a roar of defiance.

Finding another crossing would take him miles out of his way and there was no guarantee any of them would be safer.

He had the option of waiting hours or days for the waters to recede, but Yellow Horse was not a man to be deterred by something as simple as a fast water crossing. The river thundered, taunting him to brave the rumbling challenge.

Accepting the challenge, Yellow Horse squeezed the Medicine Hat with both legs. The horse sidestepped, attempting to stay out of the swiftly moving current. His rider guided is head toward the far bank, applied a spur to straighten him out, and gave the horse a slap with his quirt to urge the animal forward.

So rarely was the quirt employed, the horse surrendered his last shred of resistance and almost plunged into the cataract. He kept his feet for four or five strides, but as the water became deeper and faster moving, he lost purchase and horse and rider were swept downstream.

Knowing this would happen; Yellow Horse had started across at a point far above where he intended to emerge. Had he not done so, it was certain both he and the Medicine Hat would've drowned. Still, it was a near thing.

Yellow Horse, clinging to the horse's mane, was barely able to keep the animal's head pointed toward the far bank. The powerful mount was swimming for his life.

The horse regained his footing some seventy five yards downstream from where they'd entered, at a spot where the bank had become steeper. Another ten yards and they would've both tumbled through a narrow channel and arrived miles downstream as unrecognizable, broken and bloated flotsam.

The Medicine Hat scrambled, slipping and sliding up the muddy bank, with Yellow Horse only half on, still clinging to his mane, unable to let go.

At the top of the bank Yellow Horse regained his seat. For a moment he allowed himself to feel exhilarated. In the distance he saw buffalo, more than a dozen. Then his eyes told him what his heart refused to acknowledge. These weren't buffalo. They were longhorn cattle. The realization brought him back to the immediate situation.

Dismounting, he unsaddled the Medicine Hat and let him graze.

Usually when Yellow Horse had occasion to become so thoroughly drenched, he emerged cleaner and fresher than when he entered the water. This time, the opposite was true. His clothing was stained red, his hat was gone, and his hair and body had become a depository for coarse red silt. Even his trusted pony, which was, other than his distinctive red ears and poll, nearly white from head to toe, was now as red as the river.

Gazing down at his saddle he discovered his slicker, bedroll, and reata were missing. The saddle strings had broken and been washed away with their charges.

"*Probably swept clear on down to Louisiana,*" Yellow Horse thought.

He was thankful to still have his rifle, pistol, knife and the canteen. He'd need that last item to wash the silt out of his eyes and mouth.

Yellow Horse drew his pistol and cocked it. Just as he'd feared, the action was sluggish and gritty feeling. Both of his guns would have to be disassembled and cleaned.

At least the sun was shining and there was ample brush and firewood nearby. He'd get a fire going and start cleaning his weapons while he dried out. He needed the fire to help alleviate the chill he felt after the emersion in the cold river.

As he worked, he reflected on what he'd seen at the ruins of the settlement.

The storm had removed all trace of the men who'd fled in this direction, but his trained eyes saw things in the rubble other people would not notice.

He was more convinced than ever the massacre was not the work of any of his people. He felt certain it had been done by white men, but it was so senseless and wanton, he could scarcely believe any human beings were responsible.

CHAPTER 4

When the men returned from watering the horses, and hitching them back to the coach, they climbed back inside. Lucy noticed one man was missing.

To her surprise, the driver called out and, with a crack of the whip, the coach jolted forward. A moment later they sloshed across the creek.

"Pardon me, sir. I'm sorry I don't know your name. It appears the gentleman who was sitting across from me didn't rejoin us. May I ask what became of him?"

The man nodded, stroking his bushy mustache. The knuckles of his hand were scuffed and bruised.

"Yes, Ma'am," he replied with a tip of his hat. "My name's Thompson, Ben Thompson. The man you refer to is no gentleman. He decided to walk the remaining distance. He and I discussed it some. He came to feel a healthy hike would serve to prolong his useless life. May I ask your name?"

"I'm Lucy Meadows. Allow me to introduce Mr. and Mrs. Andrews."

"...Pleased to meet you folks. Say, there're three of you crowded together over there. Mr. Andrews, why don't you sit next to me? That way the ladies will have a little more breathing room.

"Yes sir, Mr. Thompson, I believe I will. Thank you.

As the men shifted about, Lucy observed Mr. Thompson wore a gun belt with a holstered revolver slanted grip forward over his left hip.

Seeing her interest in the matter, Ben Thompson addressed it.

"I'm sorry, Miss Meadows. I hope my weapon doesn't give you cause for alarm."

"No, Mr. Thompson. I've seen many men wearing them. My father is an officer in the United States Army. I've just not seen them carried so commonly by civilians as seems to be the normal condition out here in the west."

"This part of the country is wild and free, ma'am. Civilization and law ain't as common here as they are in—was it Maryland? Please excuse me, I couldn't help overhearing.

Out here, on any given day, a man may find himself in immediate need, whether that need is shooting game, defending his life against wanton outlaws or fighting off marauding Indians on the war path."

"I see. Surely we'll have no need to do any of those things here inside the coach."

"Perhaps not at the moment, but things could change—as they often do. Besides, in my line of work, it pays to be careful."

"What line of work is that, Mr. Thompson?"

"Presently, I'm a saloon keeper. Life being what it is, I've been in several shooting scrapes, off and on. Let's just say I have enemies, and I don't intend to let them have me."

"Mr. Thompson, are you aware you've injured your hand? What happened?"

The man nodded again.

"I scuffed um both up, a bit. When we were watering the team, I had a little trouble with an ignorant ass."

"I thought the team was made up entirely of horses."

"Yes ma'am, it surely is."

Before Lucy could respond, Bucky Andrews chimed in.

"Other than the odd hunting trip, I've never had occasion to carry a firearm. It seems like it would be cumbersome and inconvenient."

Ben Thompson smiled at him.

"We all have our burdens to bear, Mr. Andrews. For me, it's less inconvenient than being dead."

***

When the stage drew to a stop at the depot in Wichita Falls, Lucy found her-self standing on a boardwalk as the baggage was being unloaded.

"Hotel's across the street there folks," the driver said. "Saloon's right next door. Hey, lady, where do you want these trunks to go?"

It took her a moment to realize the driver was speaking to her.

"Oh, I'm going on to Fort Sill, first thing tomorrow. I won't need them tonight."

"OK. They'll hold um for you overnight here at the depot."

Lucy looked around at the rawboned town. It was hardly more than a main street and a couple of dozen buildings mostly built of wood. Her eyes came to rest across the muddy street at the front of the hotel. It was a simple, two story clapboard building with a false front.

"Is there another hotel?"

"Uhh, sure there's others, but nothing suitable for a lady. This is the one you want."

"I see. There's not much to this town, is there?"

"Oh, don't worry yourself, dearie. It may not look like much but it's a pretty nice town. Bucky and me like it well enough. The hotel has a decent kitchen and you can get hot water if you want a bath. It'll cost you three bits, but it beats the alternatives." Mrs. Andrews said. She lowered her voice.

"You'll want to avoid going out on the street after dark. Speaking of avoiding things, you should stay away from that Ben Thompson, too."

"Why is that? He seems like a gentleman."

"Humpf, maybe so, but he's a dangerous man. In these parts he's known as a gunman. Now come along. Bucky, take Miss Meadows' bag. Watch your step, dearie."

***

The next morning, as Lucy left the hotel, a tall man in the uniform of the United States Cavalry greeted her on the boardwalk.

Removing his hat, he said, "Pardon me, ma'am. I'm Lieutenant Fitzpatrick. I'm looking for a young lady named Meadows, Lucy Meadows. Might you be she?"

With a slight curtsy, she replied, "Indeed I am, Lieutenant. To what do I owe the honor of making your acquaintance?"

"I'm to escort you...that is to say...*we've* been assigned to escort the stage to Fort Sill."

"I see. Am I such valuable cargo?"

"No, ma'am, er, I mean, yes ma'am, or rather...the coach is carrying mail and other valuables, in addition to you.

Lucy tried to hide her smile behind her gloved hand.

"Well then, Lieutenant, why have you sought me out?"

"Ma'am?"

"If escorting the coach is a routine assignment, why did you come looking for me?"

"Orders, ma'am."

"I beg your pardon?"

"Your father, that is to say, the Colonel, ordered me to see to your safety and comfort, ma'am."

"Please stop calling me ma'am. Do I look like an old lady?"

"No, ma'am, I mean…Miss Meadows."

Lucy showed the Lieutenant her best smile.

"That's better, Lieutenant."

"May I assist you with your luggage, Miss Meadows?"

"I only have the one small valise. The rest of my luggage is at the stage depot. I do hope it's been loaded on the coach."

Picking up the valise and taking her arm, the soldier replied, "We'll make sure of it, ma'am, I mean, Miss Meadows."

At the depot, Lucy met the new couple who would be joining them on the last leg of the journey.

"I'm Lee Jones and this is my wife Alice. Who art thee?"

"I'm Lucy Meadows and these are my friends, Mr. and Mrs. Andrews."

"We are pleased to meet thee. To where art thee traveling, today?"

"We're only going as far as Spanish Fort." Mrs. Andrews said.

"I'm going on to Fort Sill, in the Indian Territory." Lucy added.

"Did thee say thy name is Lucy Meadows? Art thee the daughter of Colonel Meadows?"

"Yes, I am. Do you know my father?"

"We do. I am an Indian Agent assigned to assist our friends in residence on the reservation."

"Oh, I see. This is my first time out west. It seems as if everyone I meet is from somewhere else. You don't sound like you were born and raised in this part of the country. Where are you from?"

Lucy hoped she wasn't being rude, but she was very curious about the odd way Mr. Jones spoke.

Mrs. Jones laughed.

"We're westerners, Miss Meadows. Lee and I were both born and raised in Saint Louis. Thou has observed our manner of speaking differs from thine."

"Umm, yes. I hope I've not offended you."

"Not at all, we're used to it. We're members of the Society of Friends, sometimes called Quakers."

"Oh, I see."

"We would not have thee misunderstand us. Does our manner of speech confuse thee?"

"No, I've heard of Quakers, but this is the first time I've been fortunate enough to meet any."

"Thy father is looking forward to seeing thee, Miss Meadows. He speaks of thee often." Mr. Jones said.

"Does he? Oh. I'm so pleased to hear it. We haven't seen each other in years. Not since he came west. Please call me Lucy."

"The love of the Father is not diminished by the passage of time, Lucy."

"No? I feel as if I hardly know him anymore."

"He loveth thee much."

"Thank you, for saying so.

"Thou may call me, Alice, Lucy. Let's be friends."

"Hello, Alice. I can't tell you how happy I am to meet both of you. Now, please tell me all about my father."

CHAPTER 5

There were five canvas teepees on the plain below the rocky hill Yellow Horse rode down. Children played and women could be seen doing the routine camp chores.

Seeing him approach, one of the women spoke to a child who ran into a nearby teepee.

Quanah Parker, carrying a rifle and dressed in buckskins, emerged from his lodge. The child was peering around from behind him.

When Yellow Horse rode to a stop in front of Quanah Parker, He didn't expect to find the man laughing.

"What happened to you? Your horse looks like a sorrel, and you like something that crawled out of the ground. At first I didn't even recognize you. Have you come back from the dead?"

Yellow Horse grinned. It was good to hear someone speaking to him in Comanche.

"No. I just made a poor decision, and you know how hard it is to keep a white horse clean."

"Ah, I see. Are you sure you have not become a medicine man like Isa-tai? Perhaps you are starting a new ceremonial ritual. Instead of the Sun Dance, have you brought us the dirt dance?"

"No. I don't think swimming across the river, after a heavy rain during the first full moon of spring, will become popular."

"You don't know. Stranger things have happened."

Yellow Horse grinned again.

"They have, but I don't recommend doing that. How are you, Quanah?"

"I am well. My wives take good care of me. The land sustains us—as always. How are you, Yellow Horse?"

"I am well."

Quanah called to one of the older children.

"If this man ever gets off his horse, unsaddle it, and stake it out on good grass next to mine.

Yellow Horse took the hint and stepped down, handing the reins to the boy.

"You haven't asked me why I'm here, Quanah."

"You will tell me when you are ready. If not, I already know. I've been expecting you. The Great Spirit has sent you as an answer to my prayers."

Yellow Horse was stunned by the statement.

"We must speak of this."

"We will, but this is no way to welcome you. Let's get you cleaned up and put some food in your belly. Come into my lodge."

***

When the food had been cleared away, the women left the two men to talk. Yellow Horse was now dressed in buckskins. His clothes were being washed by the women.

"Someday soon, we should go to the fort and get you some things at the sutler's store. Tonight we will speak of things that matter." Quanah said.

"You've made a good life here. I appreciate your hospitality, Quanah."

"You are always welcome here, Yellow Horse. I apologize for this lodge. It is not as big as I used to have. The soldiers supplied the canvas to build the teepees, but canvas doesn't hold the warmth in winter, or keep out the rain, like buffalo hide does. In a big storm like the one we just had, the canvas leaks so much, I've been afraid it would put out the fire. My wives complain, but there is little I can do. I don't know how I will replace the robes and rugs when they are worn out."

Yellow Horse did not reply.

"Since they will no longer let us follow the great migration, perhaps I will build a house like the white people have. If I do, it will be as big and strong as any of theirs.

Like you, I am learning the way of the white man. I speak a little of their language. I even have a set of white man clothes I put on when we go to the fort." Quanah pointed to where a bowler hat sat atop a pile of folded clothing.

Yellow Horse nodded, thinking about how Quanah was adapting to this new way of life.

Quanah studied Yellow Horse for a moment.

"Those buckskins suit you. How long has it been?"

"How long has it been since I wore buckskins? I don't recall, exactly. I suppose not since the surrender."

"You have lived longer in the white man's world than anyone I know, yet I see you. I see you, Yellow Horse. You are Comanche."

"Of course, Quanah, what else would I be?"

"Christian."

"No, I do not follow the way of the cross. The old ways are the best ways."

"So you say, but I am learning to be a Christian. That too is an old way."

"Perhaps, but when they tried to make me a Christian I didn't let them."

"That was when you were a child. You were clinging to the old ways out of fear."

"Fear? I prefer to think it was strength. As a boy I drew my strength from the Great Spirit. I still do. He speaks to me through earth, water, wind and fire. I have no need of the Christian way. So long as I have the sky above me, the earth beneath me, and life giving water in the four directions, why should I become a Christian?"

"It is a way of peace. We must live in peace with the white man."

"This I am doing."

Quanah nodded.

The two men sat quietly and watched the fire for a moment. After a time, Quanah looked at Yellow Horse.

"Tell me again what happened to you when you were taken from our people."

"You know most of it. When none of the white families would claim me, I was sent to the east, to a place called a foundlings home. It was run by the Roman Catholic Church.

The women all wore the exact same costume. They were called nuns or sisters, but they weren't related to each other. The sisters were not unkind, but in some ways they were crueler than our women. They worshipped images, one of a woman and another of a man being tortured."

"Jesus."

"Yes. They tried to make me worship the images, but I wouldn't do it."

"Jesus was a man, not just some carved image."

"Yes, I know. He would've made a good Comanche. He sacrificed himself for his people. Is this not our way?"

"It is, but he was also much more."

"Yes, he was a brave man.. Like a great Comanche warrior, Jesus did not cry out, no matter what they did to him. They stripped him, beat him, and whipped him till his flesh was ripped from his body. The even nailed him to a tree, and he never cried out."

"I think you are missing the point."

"The point is, I didn't stop being Comanche, no matter what they did to me."

"Did the white people abuse you in some way?"

"No, the nuns were caring in most ways, although they were very strict about teaching us our lessons. They only beat me because I wouldn't worship the images."

"Tell me again, what was it like where they lived?"

"It was a large house, built of wood…

"What I mean is—what was the country like?"

"The house was in a city. Thousands of people lived there, more than the largest village of our people, more even than when we gathered with other tribes for pow wows.

There were so many buildings I couldn't see the land until I ran away. There are forests there, like those near us over in the direction of the sunrise, but most of the land was being farmed. The white people love to dig up the earth. Every time I ran away, they caught me and sent me back."

"Yes, I remember you telling me. You were nearly grown when you returned to our people. Listen to me, Yellow Horse. I want you to forget the pain of the past. Open your heart and your mind to the opportunities offered today, and the possibilities of hope for the future."

"Hope for the future? I don't live in some imaginary tomorrow. Today is the only day we have."

"Then let's speak of today."

They sat in silence for a time until Quanah returned to the conversation, changing the subject.

"I like the Christians here. The Indian Agent and his wife are called Quakers. They are very honest and peaceful people. We are friends."

Yellow Horse gave the slightest nod of his head.

"My friend John Sage is a Christian. He may be the only one I know. Many of the whites call themselves Christians, but they are not even decent human beings. They lie and break their promises. They are without shame.

What good is it to call yourself Christian, if you do not seek the face of the Creator? They speak of Jesus, but do not know him or follow his example. It is not for me."

"Do you seek the face of the Creator, Yellow Horse?"

"Yes, I have always done this. You say the Great Spirit sent me here in answer to your prayers. That may be so.

Living with the white men, in that life, it is not easy to know what a man should do. I want to serve our people, but when I am among the white men it is not a simple thing to hear the voice of Creator.

At the time of the half moon, I went away and found a high place to fast and pray. After three days, I was given a vision. I am here because of this vision given to me by the Great Spirit. In my vision, I saw this camp. You were in my vision, Quanah. You were calling to me. I would've come sooner, but my duties with the Rangers delayed me."

"The Great Spirit has spoken."

"What does this mean? What have you been praying about?"

"I need a man I can trust to do a thing. Among the men around here, there are few I can trust and none of those who can be trusted have the skills I require.

"What skills are those, Quanah?

"The ability to represent me in a negotiation with white men, overcome hardship and danger without fear, and protect my interests. I need a man who will get the job done."

Yellow Horse looked Quanah in the eye.

"Then, the Great Spirit *has* answered your prayers. I am your man."

"It is so."

CHAPTER 6

Travelling north on the most rugged road yet, as much rock as it was dirt, the stagecoach bounced through a broken land of exposed granite and thickets of mesquite and cedar. Lucy couldn't imagine a more bleak landscape.

"Mr. and Mrs. Jones, Miss Meadows, we're approaching Fort Sill." Lieutenant Fitzpatrick called from outside, where he rode his horse beside the vehicle.

Excited to finally be at the end of the journey, Lucy stuck her head out the window to see ahead.

The coach slowed as it reached the outskirts of the fort.

Lucy expected to see a high stockade fence of sharpened logs with watchtowers built onto the corners. Instead, she found herself looking at a scattering of conical shaped canvas tents on ground so rocky, other than scrub brush, it was devoid of vegetation. It was almost as if something had burned away all the prairie grass and every other form of healthy growing thing, leaving the raw earth trampled into hard packed mud. The exposed rock was like bits of bone showing through a wound. Tree stumps with the limbs broken off and the bark ripped away stood like bleached and twisted skeletons, remnants of another time.

The air was thick with wood smoke and other more unpleasant odors.

The number of people sitting or standing around watching the stage as it passed was astonishing. There were dozens of men, women, and children blankly staring at the people in the coach. To Lucy's further amazement, everyone she saw appeared to be some sort of Indian.

Seeing the startled look on Lucy's face, Alice Jones reached forward and touched her hand.

"Is this the first time thee has seen the native people?"

"Oh, uhh, no, I've just never seen so many all at one time. How many are there?"

"The Indian Territory is currently home to the Comanche, Kiowa, Cheyenne, Caddo, Tonkawa and Cherokee peoples, and many more. Here at this fort, these friends thee see are mostly Comanche and Kiowa." Agent Jones replied.

"Do you mean to tell me they live here, like this?"

"Thou are correct."

"Why are they living in tents and mud huts?"

"These friends are dependent on the government to supply their daily bread. They choose to stay close to the fort."

"That's horrible"

"We do what we can for them, as God provides. These thee see in misery are but a few. Most choose to live away from the fort."

"This is unacceptable. We should be ashamed. Is there something I can do to help these people? I mean it. Please call on me if there's anything I can do."

Before the Indian Agent could reply, they passed by the sentries at the gates and entered the compound of Fort Sill.

In contrast to the abject poverty they'd just seen, here, everything was in order and well maintained. The fort was laid out in blocks with proper streets lined with buildings built of stone and brick. The few people on the streets, other than the soldiers in uniform, were well dressed in the latest fashion.

To the left side of the coach, a huge parade ground came into view, on the right, a row of official looking buildings.

When the stage stopped, there was another surprise. A band struck up a lively tune.

"Do you always get a greeting like this when you return to the fort, Mr. Jones?"

"No, Lucy, this welcome was arranged for thee, by thy father."

In a moment, Lieutenant Fitzpatrick, now on foot, appeared at the door. He offered Lucy his hand.

Looking up, she saw her father in full dress uniform standing front and center at the top of some stairs on a covered porch. Behind him other officers were standing at parade rest.

Lucy accepted Lieutenant Fitzpatrick's offered hand and stepped down from the coach. The moment her feet touched the ground, the officers on the porch all snapped to attention. The band continued playing.

Not knowing what else to do. Lucy allowed the young lieutenant to escort her up the stairs. When they arrived on the porch, the band ceased playing. Lieutenant Fitzpatrick snapped to attention, saluting Colonel Meadows.

Returning the salute, her father said, "Report, Lieutenant."

"Sir. Yes, sir. Please allow me to present Miss Lucy Meadows, the Colonel's daughter."

"Thank you, Lieutenant. That will be all."

Lieutenant Fitzpatrick saluted again and turned on his heel to go back down the stairs. As he did so, two things happened. The band struck up another tune and her father opened his arms, grinning at her.

"Welcome to Fort Sill, Lucy." He said.

Lucy curtsied and replied, "Thank you, Colonel."

Her father allowed a flicker of disappointment to show on his face before removing his hat and stepping forward to take her hand.

"Don't you have a kiss for your father, baby girl?"

Lucy couldn't help herself. She rushed into his arms, hot tears threatening to spoil the moment.

***

After all the introductions were made, Lucy and Colonel Meadows walked down the street to her father's house in the area designated as the officer's quarters.

Much like the other houses on the block, his was an unremarkable but tidy, single story house, built of stone. There was a covered porch across the front, on which two high backed wooden chairs with a table between them and a porch swing completed the homey feel.

Inside, the front room was large and tastefully decorated. The walls were plastered and painted. The furniture was of good quality and polished to perfection. Two overstuffed chairs and a couch, all of them covered in matching velvet, were arranged in front of a huge fireplace. A buffalo hide was laid down as a rug on the cobblestone floor. Against one wall, a mahogany writing desk reminded Lucy of her father's rare correspondence.

All in all, while it wasn't as grand as the house in which she'd grown up in Maryland, it was much finer than she'd expected.

"Oh my, this is not at all the way I imagined the fort would be."

"I'm sorry, Lucy. Life out here is harsh and I know the conditions are more austere than those to which you are accustomed. I hope you're not too disappointed."

"No, sir, it's not that at all. In my mind I'd pictured a frontier outpost like this, to be a log fort, and you'd be living in a single room with a dirt floor."

Her father laughed.

"These are modern times, Lucy, and this is a modern fort. We make out all right. Let me show you to your room."

CHAPTER 7

"What would you have me do, Quanah?" Yellow Horse asked.

Quanah studied him for a moment. It was as if he were trying to see into the other man's soul. As he looked his friend in the eye, he explained his thinking.

"The white man values wealth. To them, the accumulation of money, and believing they own things, is sacred. You know this better than I do. Tell me, Yellow Horse, what do the Comanche own? What is sacred to us?"

"I believe we own nothing. All that we have is a gift from the Creator, given to us in trust. We Comanche value our life on the Comancheria, the bison herds and wildlife on the earth that sustains us, the water that gives us life, our families and our freedom. These things are sacred to us."

"This is so, but like you, I must learn to live in the white man's world. Every herd that comes up the trail pays me in cattle for the privilege of crossing our reservation. These are mostly steers. The best of them I give to our people. The rest I fatten and sell in Kansas. I will use the money to buy breeding stock."

"Will they let you do this?"

"The Agent told me the government wants us to use the land and make a living on it."

"Why cattle?"

"What do we have here on the reservation?"

"There is nothing here. The United States claims they own everything."

"Not everything. We have grass, good grass. We have prairie grass farther than the eye can see in each of the four directions. The Creator owns the grass.

I will raise cattle on the Creator's grass. I'll breed a great many cattle and sell them to the white people for money. Today, many whites have their cattle grazing in the Indian Territory. This should not be so. Maybe I'll choose which white people graze their cattle here, for a price.

I'll use what the Creator has for us in this place to earn the white man's money. A man with money can become important in the white man's world. Is this not so?"

Yellow Horse was astonished. Quanah possessed a kind of wisdom he himself lacked.

"Yes. It is so. You have the heart and soul of a Comanche, Quanah, but you are learning to think like a white man."

"It is as it must be. If we can no longer continue in the old ways, we must learn another way."

"Why do you live so far from the fort?"

"They don't like me to have so many wives. They want me to have no more than three. Can you believe that?"

"Yes, most of them would be offended by more than even one wife. So, what they don't see won't bother them? Is that the idea?"

Quanah grinned.

"That and I like living in the old way. Some things I will not let them take from me."

"I too, prefer the old ways."

"There is a place for you here on the reservation. You will soon be thirty years old. Why don't you settle down and raise a family, Yellow Horse? There are suitable women among us, some who have eyes for you."

Before answering, Yellow Horse stared into the fire for a moment.

"No. I value my freedom too much. I spend most of my time in the lonely places and wastelands—our homeland. I live without the white man's boundaries. I travel far and wide. Life on the reservation is not for me."

"You live with the Rangers. You help them enforce the white man's law. How is there freedom in that?"

"Freedom must be found inside us. I am true to the way the Great Spirit made me. The Rangers are warriors. Even the Comanche respect them for that. Scouting for the Rangers is the only way I can continue to live as a warrior. That is my freedom."

"Tu-ukumah is also a warrior. I tried to get him to stay here on the reservation. He does not understand. The only way we can survive as a people is by learning to live in peace with the whites.

He wants to purge the buffalo hunters from the Comancheria. Tu-ukumah will fail, and pay a great price for making war on the hunters. Here, he could be free. Out there, he will be hunted down, beaten and brought back in chains. We cannot defeat the white man by making war. That time is behind us.

The Quakers tell me that one day the time for warriors will pass away altogether. It has passed for me."

Yellow Horse nodded.

"I am not Tu-ukumah. My days of fighting the white man are no more. I too know there are seasons in life, but I am not living in the same season as you are, Quanah. If I were, you would not have need of me."

It was Quanah's turn to nod.

"It is so."

"In the morning I will ride to the fort." Yellow Horse said.

"I cannot go with you. The Colonel is paying me a formal visit. I must show him every courtesy and hospitality. We need to get his permission to buy cattle in Texas. You could stay here and talk to him."

"No, I have Ranger business at the fort. I must report to Captain Lee.

On the third night of the week before the full moon, several people were murdered at a settlement across the river in Texas. After they burned the place, the killers came here, to the Territory.

"The whites will blame us." Quanah said.

"How do you know none of our people did it?"

"I would hear of it. There has been no word, until now."

"I believe it was done by white renegades. They killed everyone, men, women and children. They went there to do that, and to steal everything they had. Their horses were shod with iron."

"No, this was not done by our people."

Also, I must tell Captain Lee, Dutch Henry Bourne escaped with the two dozen mules he stole from the army supply train sent down here from Kansas.

Quanah chuckled.

"Now, *that* is something I have in common with Dutch Henry. I've done it myself, many times."

Yellow Horse smiled and shrugged in response.

"This thing across the river, the massacre worries me. Whoever did it, they will do it again. You're right; the whites will think we are responsible," he said.

"How many men did this thing?"

"I can't be sure. The rains washed away their tracks."

"So, you don't even know for sure they came here."

"I believe they did."

The two men stared into the fire for a moment.

"Perhaps they've fled all the way to Kansas." Quanah said.

"You must keep a watch. Tell the army if you see or hear of any white men hiding on the reservation."

"There are many. White thieves and killers are like leaves blown in from the four directions. If they are hidden among the other nations, I might not hear of it."

"These are not common outlaws. They don't care who they kill. Your family is not safe this far from the fort."

"We are not alone. I have cattle and men watching over them. The army patrols through here. Bad men will not want to come near us."

"I hope you're right."

"The Great Spirit will protect us and see justice is done."

"All things considered, I'm not so sure."

Quanah studied Yellow Horse for a moment.

"You have too much pain. You struggle against the changes. Changes are a normal part of life. We do not see the tree growing, but it grows. The river alters course, but we do not have eyes to see when and where it will happen. So it is with all things under the sky. The Creator has a plan for all of his people, but we seldom see or understand it. Is this not so, Yellow Horse?"

Yellow Horse nodded his agreement.

"Yes, Quanah, this is so."

"When the storm winds blow, the tree that does not bend will be broken. Each season must give way to the next. We must accept these things as they happen. This is why, even when we do not see or understand, we must remain faithful. Is this not so?"

Yellow Horse bowed his head. He was not able to speak.

"Do not let the events of life knock you down or steal your faith. The Creator knows your need, and He will direct your paths. You must not doubt or lose courage."

Yellow Horse looked up at Quanah.

"These words speak to me." He said.

Quanah slapped him on the shoulder.

"They should, I say them to myself, all the time."

DAN ARNOLD

CHAPTER 8

Colonel Meadows was sipping brandy and smoking a cigar as he and Lucy were sitting out on the porch after supper. He glanced over at Lucy.

"Tomorrow, if you're up for an adventure, there's someone I'd like you to meet."

"Really, how is meeting someone supposed to be an adventure?"

I want you to meet a man named Quanah Parker. He's the primary leader of the Comanche. I thought we'd take a drive out to his camp. It's about an hour's ride north of here."

"OK, that sounds like fun. Why do you want me to meet the gentleman?"

"At supper you were telling us how sad it makes you to see the Indians struggling to learn our ways. Chief Parker is something of a success story. He's making a real effort to adjust to our way of life. If he's able to convince his people to follow his example, there's hope for the future."

"That's wonderful. Tell me all about him."

"...Where to begin? Quanah Parker is one of the most colorful and interesting men I've ever met. He's lived the savage life of the untamed Indian on the plains. Up until two years ago, we were at war with each other, a war that started when the first Spaniards arrived on the plains nearly three hundred years ago.

When we first met, he spoke no English, only Comanche and sign language. That wouldn't be surprising except for the fact he's half white."

Lucy's eyes got bigger as her eyebrows shot up.

"That's right; his mother was a white woman, captured as a child and raised as a Comanche. By the time Quanah was learning to speak, she probably hadn't spoken a word of English in many years. Besides, she was re-captured and taken away by the Texas Rangers while Quanah was still a boy.

Quanah's father was a great war Chief named Peta Nocona. He died of wounds he sustained in combat. Quanah had cause to hate white people and fight for his freedom, from an early age.

For the last two years, since the surrender, Chief Parker's been living north of here on West Cache Creek. He's completely self-sufficient. Not only that, he has abundance enough to provide for the needs of many of his people. He's learning English and even dresses like a white man when he visits the fort.

"That's wonderful, has he become a Christian?"

"That's difficult to say. It's not for me to judge. He spends a fair amount of time with the Indian Agent and his wife. They're Quakers, you know."

"I came in on the same stagecoach with them. I really like Alice."

"That's right, you did. Mr. Jones tells me Chief Parker is trying to learn what Christianity is all about."

Aren't we all?" Lucy said, with a smile.

"In Quanah's case, it's quite a bit more challenging. He's completely unfamiliar with our culture and he has very little English."

"And, the way Quakers speak…"

"Sure, there's that. Still, Chief Parker understands English better than he can speak it. He's asked us to start a school for the children here on the reservation, so they will have a better opportunity to learn our ways."

"That's a wonderful idea."

"It is, but it's up to Mr. Jones and the other Indian Agents to arrange for the funding. It's not the army's responsibility."

"I'd think the government would understand how important it is for children, especially these children, to get an education."

"Perhaps, but getting anything out here takes a very long time. The more bureaucracy involved, the longer it takes."

"I could teach them."

Colonel Meadows closed his eyes, rubbing his forehead with the hand holding the cigar. He took a sip of brandy before answering.

"Lucy, there are hundreds of children just in this area near the fort, probably several thousand on the reservation."

"Oh, I hadn't thought of that."

"You need to learn something about the Indians."

"What's that?"

"No, I mean you know almost nothing about them. I think a visit to Chief Parker's camp might be the perfect place to start. I've sent word we'll be there in the morning."

***

Rank has its privileges, and as the ranking officer at Fort Sill, Colonel Meadows never traveled without an escort. Since Lucy was traveling with him, they rode together in a carriage.

Their escort consisted of Lieutenant Fitzpatrick, an Apache scout, four mounted troopers and a driver.

Where men on foot or mounted cavalry could travel cross country, wagons and other wheeled conveyances had to choose more circuitous routes to avoid cedar thickets, rocky promontories, narrow defiles and steep ravines.

Over time, Quanah had developed a wagon route between his camp and the fort. It added a couple of miles to the journey, but afforded a safe and well defined trail.

From her seat in the carriage, the Wichita Mountains appeared to be little more than monumental piles of giant boulders. The Indian Territory was the rockiest and most desolate country she'd ever seen. From her perspective it was all rocks, steep grades or yawning ravines.

Since her arrival at Fort Sill, the wind had never stopped blowing. It seemed as if on any given day, it could be a gentle breeze, brisk and gusty, or a howling gale. Some days it achieved all of those in the same hour. The wind moaned, whistled, or rustled, but was almost never silent.

She'd heard stories about women alone in the west going mad from the never ending sound of the wind. While she was aware of it and found it tiresome on occasion, it didn't cause her any anxiety.

"If Mr. Parker is becoming so civilized, do we really need all these soldiers with us?"

"It's always better to be safe than sorry, Lucy. The Indian Territory is a place where desperate men flee the law, and some of the Indians still aren't too picky about who they steal horses from. It also happens that as an important man, Chief Parker would expect me to travel with an escort."

"What about the scout? It seems to me this wagon route is pretty easy to follow."

"Right, but he speaks Comanche. We don't. He'll be more useful as an interpreter than a scout."

"You said Chief Parker is learning to speak English."

"We'll see. We're coming up on his camp now."

Topping out on the side of a granite strewn elevation, they had an unobstructed view of the camp below them.

To one side of a wide meadow with a creek running through it, near a corral with half a dozen horses in it, three covered wagons were parked side by side.

As unremarkable as that was, the sight of five large canvas teepees seemed incongruous.

The teepees were arranged in a circle, each facing east. Between them, a large fire pit was equipped for cooking. There were barrels and boxes in sight, and a huge table with what appeared to be at least two dozen chairs around it.

Everywhere Lucy looked, women and children were bustling about, evidently preparing for their visit.

"It looks like Chief Parker invited a bunch of his people to meet us." Lucy said.

Her dad looked at her and winked.

"Well not exactly, Lucy. You're in for a surprise. The adventure is just about to begin."

CHAPTER 9

Yellow Horse pulled his horse to a stop. Experience had taught him not to allow himself to be silhouetted against the skyline. From his position on the hillside, he and his horse were concealed behind rocks and cedars, but he was able to watch the soldiers below.

The small party was coming from the direction of Fort Sill, following the wagon road toward Quanah's encampment.

Yellow Horse recognized the officer in the carriage, but the stunning young woman seated beside him was someone he'd never seen before. Did Colonel Meadows have a daughter, or was this his wife? He would ask Quanah, later.

Old habits having served him well, Yellow Horse didn't move until the soldiers, the carriage and their scout disappeared from sight.

A short time later, he stopped again, this time to observe the fort and the village surrounding it.

Where the fort showed military order, the teepees and wickiup dwellings around it were haphazard and distressing to look upon. All the trees and nearby brush had been stripped to make poles, posts or used for firewood. The grass was gone and the ground was mostly beaten bare. Here and there were small cultivated patches showing the first attempts at planting spring crops.

How different this was from the way his people had lived as rulers of the plains. They were nomadic people.

Not so long ago, they gathered their lodge poles from high in the western mountains. Teepees were tall and wide, covered in the finest buffalo hides. Villages were divided into sections by broad avenues from the four directions. At the center was a huge teepee, used as the meeting lodge. Around it the large teepees of the principle men and their families were in close proximity, the lesser members of the village spreading out from there. They moved from one camp site to another, following the migration of the buffalo herds.

Here, the fort was the central meeting place. The surrounding dwellings were small and covered with canvas, blankets, or brush caked with mud. The women wore rags or dirty blankets. The men fared no better. A few curs and skinny livestock wandered among them. Children were in evidence, but no one was teaching them the skills they would need to be providers for their people.

With a sigh he moved his horse up into a lope, riding down the hill and onto the road to the fort.

***

Captain P.L. Lee looked up from the papers on his desk as Yellow Horse was escorted to stand in front of him.

"That'll be all, Sergeant."

"Sir? He's still armed..."

"Thank you for that word of caution, Sergeant. Like I said, that'll be all."

The sergeant tried to give Yellow Horse a dark look, but his complexion interfered. He turned on his heel and walked out of the office.

Captain Lee regarded Yellow Horse for a moment. He saw a man of average height and weight, dressed in tan canvas pants with reddish stains, a blue shirt with similar stains and a dark grey woolen vest, likewise discolored. His boots were scuffed and the only thing about the fellow that appeared to be clean was his ammunition belt and the pistol tucked into it. His complexion was darkened, but no more so than men who spent most of their time outdoors. His eyes were grey and his hair was brown. The only thing that gave away his native heritage was his long braids, tied with strips of rawhide.

"Good morning Mr. Yellow Horse. Please have a seat. May I offer you a cigar?"

Yellow Horse selected a ladder back chair and pulled it around in front of the captain's desk. He shook his head

"No thank you, Captain. I'm here to report."

"I should apologize for Sergeant Jackson's attitude. He's a stickler for the rules."

"What rules are those?"

"He didn't tell you? We don't generally allow armed, uhh, men, into this office."

"You mean, an armed Comanche, don't you?

Captain Lee shrugged.

"I heard you were scouting for the Texas Rangers. What do you want to report?"

"Seven days ago, Dutch Henry Bourne and his men stole a couple dozen mules from an army supply train coming from Kansas."

"That's a matter of record."

"Some of us from Company D were in Eagle Springs when we got word of the theft. We learned Dutch Henry was headed across the panhandle on his way to Colorado, so we cut northwest to see if we could pick up his trail and recover the army's mules. We were on his trail when the storm hit. Long story short—he and his bunch escaped."

"Did you come all the way here to tell me that?"

"No, I was coming here anyway. The more important thing I have to tell you is; some killers crossed the river from Texas, the day before yesterday."

"That's nothing new. This is the kind of thing you people do. You sneak off the reservation, attack white settlers, and then run back to the Territory begging us to protect you from the angry citizens."

"This is different."

"How's that?"

"I'm speaking of butchers. They burned down a settlement and killed every man, woman and child."

"Where did this happen?"

"A family named Morgan, two brothers, their wives and children and some other folks, started a settlement about fifteen miles north of Eagle Springs."

"Isn't that closer to Fort Griffin?"

"No, it's just the other side of the river, almost due west of here."

Captain Lee made a face.

"Sounds to me like the work of murdering savages."

"Yes, white savages."

"What makes you think it was done by white people? Could be it was some of your people. Might've been Blackhorse and his bunch."

"No, Tu-ukamah and his band is on the far side the Llano Estacado, many days ride from here."

"Are you sure about that?"

"I am."

"Why are you telling me?"

"The killers came here. My people have no defense against men like this. They depend on the army to protect them. It's my duty to inform you of what happened, so you can take appropriate measures."

"I still say it sounds like some kind of Indian raid. If that's the case, I can't help you."

"I told you, these are white men. What will you do?"

Lieutenant Lee scrubbed his face with both hands.

"Texas trash travels through here with every herd that goes up the trail. Do you have any idea how big the Indian Territory is?

These killers are probably long gone. If it was some sort of white outlaws as you say, you should bring it to the attention of the United States Marshals. But, unless you can tell them what these men look like, there's little anyone can do. Do you even know how many men conducted the attack?"

"No."

"Well then, thank you for your report. Is there anything else?"

Yellow Horse sighed and stood up. He put the chair back against the wall. As he turned and walked away, he said,

"No, Captain. That'll be all."

CHAPTER 10

"I understand thy father took thee out to meet Quanah Parker at his encampment. What did thou think of that experience?" Alice Jones asked Lucy.

"Are you asking me if I'm shocked?"

"Are thou?"

Lucy looked down and sighed.

"I was, at first. As I've come to know the women better, I've decided it doesn't matter to me."

Alice nodded thoughtfully.

"Yes, but polygamy is a sin in the eyes of God."

"I know, but what would you have them do? Chief Parker's wives and children are well cared for."

"Yes, they are. They're much better off than so many others. I believe the blood of Jesus is sufficient to cover all our sins, even in a situation like this. Still, how can Chief Parker profess to be a Christian if he continues to live in that sinful lifestyle?"

"Does he?"

"Profess himself as a Christian? I'm not sure. I don't think he has, yet. My husband tells me Chief Parker has a great curiosity on the subject."

"I imagine it's a very difficult choice for him."

Alice laughed.

"…Which part, choosing to become a Christian, or having so many wives?"

Both women giggled at the comment.

"Quanah Parker and his family are doing well. Many others are struggling to survive. The local women work so hard and have so little. Is there anything I can do to help?"

"It's an enormous challenge for us. The government doesn't consider meeting the needs of a vanquished enemy to be a high priority. My husband is frustrated. He's learned the hard way not to make any promises in his capacity as an Indian Agent. The people have plenty of blankets, but the beef supply is unreliable. Chief Parker makes sure *his* people get fed, but there are horrific shortages all across the Territory. The same goes for sundries."

"I'm sorry. I know it isn't easy. I don't have much in the way of wealth, but I want to help in any way I can."

"These are proud people. The women are skilled at making clothing out of animal hides, but for them, those are hard to come by these days. The fabric clothing doesn't hold up as well. It's become rather threadbare. Many use cut up gunny sacks, others have nothing."

Lucy's eyes lit up.

"What if I bought bolts of fabric from the sutler's store? We could distribute it to women in the area so they can make clothes for their families. Would that help?"

"Yes. It would, and because the women will make the clothing, it won't take away their dignity like accepting handout clothes from the agency does. I thank thee, Lucy. It is kind of thee."

"I only wish I could do more."

***

Lucy was on the porch when three wagons drew to a stop on the edge of the parade ground, directly in front of her father's headquarters building. She watched as women and children emerged. Evidently it was a visit from Quanah Parker's family.

Smiling, she ducked inside to grab a shawl, and her hat, before setting out to greet them.

Moments later, she laughed at the antics of the children playing in the yard. Their happy smiles and dark faces were so like those of all children everywhere. The other women were enjoying this moment as well, though in most ways they were very different from Lucy.

The children's mothers were wrapped in blankets, pulled up over their heads, partly to stay warm in these first days of spring, but mostly to shield them from the prying eyes of the white men here at Fort Sill.

In contrast, Lucy was dressed in the latest fashion. Her light blue dress accentuated her sparkling eyes. Her blond hair in ringlets, beneath her matching hat, shone like burnished gold. A knit shawl completed the outfit.

The Comanche women had quickly come to know her as a kind human being and a friend. The racial and cultural differences were of little concern to them. These were women who looked at the heart, and judged only the person's actions and attitudes. Skin color was of little importance. Indeed, their husband, Quanah Parker, the Chief of the Quahadi band of Comanche, was half white himself.

Still, at this time, in this place, the white men, especially the soldiers, were regarded by the Comanche women as enemies and threats—nothing more. The dark skinned, "Buffalo Soldiers" at Fort Sill were better liked and respected as both men and warriors.

When Lucy first came to this lonely outpost where her father was now stationed, she'd been shocked to learn all these children were Quanah's, and that all seven women were his wives.

The wild Comanche, who had never been defeated in war by the white soldiers, was becoming civilized.

"Wives say you give gingham, needles and buttons to women of my people."

Startled, Lucy gave an involuntary jump. She hadn't heard the man's approach from behind her.

She turned to see two men, not just one, standing side by side.

"Yes, Chief Parker, I hope they will be useful."

"Hmmm. Heap good."

Quanah Parker wore the business suit and bowler hat he had adopted in place of the buckskins and feathers he wore in his encampment. His long hair in braids, dark skin and fierce countenance were the only visible remnant of his tribal heritage.

The other man was similar in appearance although somewhat lighter in complexion. He had the same broad chest and thick arms, but if it weren't for his long brown hair, braided in the same fashion as Chief Parker, he could've passed for a white man. He wore work clothing that appeared to be brand new. His canvas pants were tucked into the tops of high riding boots with spurs. A white linen shirt under a wool vest, and a blue bandana completed the outfit. She couldn't help noticing his gun belt. The overall impression was like that of most of the plainsmen she'd seen.

His face was without expression, but his grey eyes scanned her from the ground up. Lucy felt herself flush under his scrutiny.

Seeing this, Quanah Parker smiled. Glancing at the man, he made the introductions.

"Him called, James Yellow Horse. Him friend, many years, mighty warrior." Looking at her he pointed. "She, Colonel Meadows' daughter, her name Lucy."

To Lucy's surprise, Mr. Yellow Horse removed his broad brimmed hat, bowed slightly and said, "Pleased to make your acquaintance, Miss Meadows."

Lucy was stunned. His refined manners and polished use of the language were not just uncommon in this savage land, but seemed incongruous coming from someone whose name, company and appearance, suggested Comanche heritage.

In comparison, while Quanah Parker was becoming more accustomed to speaking English, his use of the language was still limited.

How could this man, James Yellow Horse, be better educated? He was dressed like a white man, but hadn't Quanah Parker just said he was a Comanche brave?

"I'm pleased to meet you, Mr. Yellow Horse. Do you know my father?"

"I do." He said, his gaze unwavering.

"What brings you to Fort Sill?"

Lucy regretted the question immediately. If he *was* a Comanche, after the Buffalo War, he'd had no choice in the matter. When Quanah Parker finally surrendered in 1875, all of his people were exiled to the reservation. They'd been forced to march more than a hundred miles to the fort under heavy guard.

She felt herself flush even further.

If the man was offended by the poorly worded question, he showed no sign.

"Chief Parker wants to buy some cattle in Texas and have them driven here. I'm to be his agent. We had to get approval from both the Indian Agent and your father."

"Did you? Get approval, I mean." She stammered.

"Yes," he said, with a slight smile that made crow's feet appear at the outer corners of his eyes. "If you'll excuse us, Miss Meadows, we must be going. I hope to see you again on another occasion."

Quanah Parker had watched this exchange with some amusement evident on his bronze face.

"We go now." He clapped his hands and pointed to the wagons.

The women began rounding up the smaller children as the older ones made haste to obey.

Within minutes, all three wagons were loaded. James Yellow Horse, mounted on a mostly white colored pinto, trotted along beside the wagon driven by Quanah Parker. Two of Quanah's wives drove the others.

As the small wagon train left the compound, Lucy lifted a hand, waiving farewell.

Just as she started to turn away, Yellow Horse looked back at her and silently raised his own hand. Was the dust stirred up by the teams and wagons making her see things, or was the man smiling? Could he be smiling at her?

CHAPTER 11

Lucy told her father about her meeting with Quanah and the man called Yellow Horse. She asked about the unusually colorful horse the latter man had ridden.

"It's a type of pinto called a "Medicine Hat." The Comanche believe it's a magical beast that somehow protects it's rider in battle. They aren't common, so only the greatest warriors are allowed to have them. That particular horse was a gift from Chief Parker. He has one himself.

When we fought them in the Buffalo War, we destroyed over a thousand of their horses. So, you're right. These days it's unusual to see a Comanche mounted on a horse so prized among them."

Lucy and Colonel Meadows were sitting on the porch outside their stone walled house in the officer's quarters, shortly after supper.

He continued his narrative.

"That man Yellow Horse is a rather unusual fellow. They say he's half Comanche and half Cherokee on his mother's side. That explains his coloring. He's spent most of his life living and working among white people. That's why he's so familiar with our language and customs."

"I know many white people who have no polish whatsoever. How did he come to be so well educated and achieve such a distinguished manner?" Lucy wondered, out loud.

"I'm told, as a child he was seized in an army raid on a Comanche village. They mistook him for a kidnapped white boy. When no white people claimed him, they shipped him off to a Catholic orphanage, somewhere in the east. They gave him the name 'James" and tried to make him a Christian. He learned to speak English, read, write and do arithmetic there.

When the War Between the States broke out he was just a young teen. He ran away from the orphanage and returned to the Comancheria."

"What is that?"

"It's the homeland of the Comanche. The Comancheria spreads across thousands of square miles of plains, canyons and grasslands from here through Texas, into New Mexico and Colorado. The Indian Territory is just a small piece of the Comancheria."

"His people used to own this land?"

"The Indians don't think like we do. They believe the land cannot be owned by anyone. Whatever they think, we own it now. The Indian Territory is federal land and it's an important trade route.

The big cattle herds come through here, headed for the railroad in Kansas. They mostly come up the Chisholm Trail.

YELLOW HORSE

Your friend, Yellow Horse, was there at the beginning of the cattle industry.

A dozen years ago, right after the war between the states, a man in Texas named Charlie Goodnight and his partner, Oliver Loving, were planning to drive a herd of cattle to Colorado. They had to go right through the heart of the Comancheria.

Goodnight knew Quanah Parker, and asked if he could provide a scout and interpreter for them. Quanah sent the young James Yellow Horse."

Colonel Meadows paused to light a cigar. When it was pulling to his satisfaction, he continued his account.

"Now, this is where the story gets interesting. At some point Yellow Horse and Loving set out ahead of the herd. They were attacked by a different band of Comanche. Yellow Horse fought those Comanche, right alongside Loving. They were both wounded, but they escaped and made it to Fort Sumner, where, being Comanche, Yellow Horse was hated by the locals and nearly hung. Goodnight and the herd arrived just in time to save him from the lynch mob. Loving later succumbed to gangrene.

Yellow Horse worked for Goodnight for several years after that. He lived pretty much as a white man in those days, but when the conflict between the whites and Indians erupted into all-out war, he chose to ride with Quanah Parker and the Quahadi band of his people.

So, you see, at different times, and in different places, Yellow Horse fought on both sides. Still, he doesn't want people to think of him as a white man. No matter how polished he seems on the outside, just under the surface, he's still a wild savage who's never been tamed."

Her father took a deep breath and let it out slowly.

"But, before long, they will *all* be tamed. It's a sad thing, Lucy, to see a people beaten down like that. I'm not proud of it. Our government has decided the best way to subjugate the plains Indians is to destroy their way of life.

The Indians you see here were nomadic people whose entire life cycle was linked to the great buffalo herds.

The Indians have been impeding our westward expansion on the continent, so the decision makers in Washington have found a solution. If we wipe out the buffalo, we'll subdue the Indians. That's the thinking and that's what we're doing. Tens of millions of buffalo have already been destroyed.

Now, you have to understand, the buffalo hunters aren't solitary hunters shooting a few buffalo, here and there. No, these are organized, commercial companies of men destroying whole herds and only taking the skins. They leave the meat to rot."

Colonel Meadows ground out his cigar. The aroma had become distasteful to him. It had always been distasteful to Lucy. It made her think of burning socks.

"It is the most horrible and evil thing the Indian peoples can imagine." Her father continued. "It is so offensive, the Kiowa, Comanche and Cheyenne banded together to fight the buffalo hunters.

Just above the Canadian River there's a small trading post and watering hole for the hunters, near the same place Kit Carson fought the Comanche and Kiowa back in 1864. A place they call Adobe Walls. Knowing many of the buffalo hunters were there, one morning at dawn, a combined force of Cheyenne, Kiowa and Comanche attacked.

These are the most excellent horseman on the plains, perhaps the finest light cavalry in the world, and they outnumbered the people in Adobe Walls nearly ten to one.

I met a fellow named Bat Masterson. He was among those defending the settlement. He told me, because the buffalo hunter's Sharp's rifles were deadly at distance, and with the cover of the thick walls, the hunters were able to hold off the Indians, suffering only a few casualties.

The Indians were out in the open and outgunned.

In the fighting, Chief Parker was shot off his mount. They say Yellow Horse galloped his horse across open ground, through a hail of bullets, to rescue him.

After about three days, the raiding party realized they couldn't mount an effective attack across open ground on the people shooting from cover in Adobe Walls. Another large company of white hunters were approaching from the north. Without hope of victory, the Indians retreated.

That fight is now called the second battle of Adobe Walls. It was the beginning of the Buffalo War, and the catalyst for the total subjugation of all the Indian tribes. Our government won't stop till it's done.

That's how I got posted here. General Sheridan was ordered to put a permanent end to the uprising. We set out to make war on the Comanche, Cheyenne and Kiowa.

For several months we fought small battles and skirmishes with them all across the panhandle of Texas. They avoided us when they could. When they couldn't, they'd put up a brief fight and then disappear into the wilderness.

That's some mighty rough country. The conditions are harsh. We lost men, but they lost whole villages. We lost a few horses and mules, but we captured and killed their horses by the hundreds.

Quanah Parker and the Quahadi band were the last to abandon the fight. Yellow Horse helped negotiate the surrender. He and Goodnight arranged safe passage here for Quanah and the rest.

They're the last great warriors of the Comanche people, a proud people who ruled the plains for thousands of years.

These days, Quanah has cattle on the same grass where the great buffalo herds once roamed. I wonder how he feels about that.

Some of his people are still fighting mad. A bunch left the reservation several months ago. There's more trouble brewing. You may not be safe out here."

Lucy had never heard her father tell such a long, sad story. She figured the brandy he was sipping was loosening his tongue.

"So, Mr. Yellow Horse has been here at the fort the last couple of years, since the surrender?" She asked.

"Hmmm? Yellow Horse? No, he spends most of his time in Texas. He does some scouting for the Texas Rangers."

Lucy studied her father where he sat watching the sun as it started sliding below the far horizon. He seemed so much older and more world weary now than he had been only a few years back. Before the War Between the States, and before he was sent west with General Sheridan, he'd been more fun. Of course she'd been only a little girl back then.

She wondered if she'd changed as much in his eyes, in the years they'd been apart, as he had in hers.

Sensing her gaze, he smiled and stood up, straightening his uniform.

"Let's go in. I'd love to hear you read from the scriptures, the book of Psalms, perhaps?"

Returning the smile she took his offered arm.

"Certainly, Colonel Daddy, it will be my pleasure.

DAN ARNOLD

CHAPTER 12

As they enjoyed the morning sunshine outside his lodge, Quanah Parker and Yellow Horse discussed the ways they might obtain cattle.

"Tell me again why you won't buy a herd from one of the drives going north to the railroad? Most of the big herds pass right through the Territory."

"Those are mostly steers bound for slaughter. The trail bosses have no respect for us. They remember how we stampeded their herds so we could steal cattle when they wouldn't pay the toll to cross the Comancheria. All of them resent having to give us cattle in exchange for permission to pass through the reservation. I don't need more steers. I need strong breeding stock.

These herds you speak of are all coming from Texas. The Army won't trust us to leave the Territory to round up wild cattle. We'll have to buy them. Texas is the best place to buy good cattle at a reasonable price. Who do you know in Texas that would sell cattle to me?"

Yellow Horse rubbed the edge of his jaw with the knuckles of his right hand.

"I've been thinking about it. You know Charles Goodnight. I think he might sell good breeding stock to you."

"Goodnight, the Ranger? He was a fierce enemy in the old days. I know you and your friend John Sage took several herds up the trail for him, but that was before you and I made war on the buffalo hunters. Will he sell to me?"

"It is true, he was an enemy in the old days, but he hasn't been a Ranger for many years. He's been as good a friend as he was a foe."

"He did speak for us when we surrendered. Yes, go to him, see if he will sell me good breeding stock. If not, we will find another."

"I will leave tomorrow."

"It is good."

Yellow Horse nodded.

"I won't return without a herd. When I come, you must be ready to pay up. There will be men with me who must be paid."

"How soon will you return?"

"If Goodnight will help us, I will be back in a week or ten days. If I must ride farther..." Yellow Horse shrugged.

"I have the money now. There will be no delay in paying."

"It is good."

The two men sat and watched the clouds drift across the horizon. After a time, Yellow Horse spoke first.

"Tell me about the young woman, the daughter of Colonel Meadows. I noticed her on the day she and her father came to visit you. When I met her yesterday, I was impressed. She is not afraid of us."

Quanah chuckled.

"That is what impressed you? She is not afraid of us? You do not even know yourself. I saw how you looked at her."

Yellow Horse scowled.

"Well, she is striking. Naturally I noticed that, but there is something else about her. She has a good heart."

"She is a Christian."

"No, that can't be it. The nuns were Christians. She is different, not like them."

Quanah squinted at Yellow Horse.

"I tell you to settle down with a good Comanche woman. You tell me you're not ready. Now you tell me you're infatuated with the Colonel's daughter?"

"What? No. I'm just curious about her."

Quanah snorted.

Yellow Horse ignored him.

"I think I will ride back to the fort. Maybe I can strike up a conversation with her."

Quanah held up a hand.

"Be careful. She is not for you. The Colonel would not approve of his daughter getting involved with a Comanche."

"Who said anything about getting involved? I've just never met anyone quite like her."

"Sure, that's how it starts."

"Don't worry. I doubt a white woman would have any interest in a Comanche."

"Should I remind you? My mother was a white woman."

"I know, but your mother was raised as a Comanche."

"She was still a white woman, who loved my father."

"Now, who said anything about love? Besides, did you see her useless hat, and those silly shoes she was wearing? That woman lacks good sense. Lucy Meadows is as out of place here as a lodge pole pine on the Llano Estacado. I'm going to the fort. I'll be back before dark."

As Yellow Horse rode away, Quanah looked up at the sky.

"What more could I have done, Great Father? I tried to warn him. He says Lucy Meadows lacks good sense. Now, we will see which of them is the more foolish."

**

Yellow Horse dismounted outside the sutler's store. As he secured the Medicine Hat to a hitching rail, he observed two women approaching from farther down the street. One of the women was Lucy Meadows.

The women were talking too intently to notice him, until they were only a few steps away.

Looking up first, Lucy recognized his horse, then she stopped walking as she and Yellow Horse locked eyes on each other.

Yellow Horse smiled.

To his delight, the smile was returned.

"Hello, Mr. Yellow Horse. Do you know Alice Jones, the wife of the Indian Agent?"

Yellow Horse removed his hat, holding it with both hands.

"Hello, Miss Meadows. No, we've not met. How do you do, Mrs. Jones?"

Alice Jones hadn't missed the interaction between the two.

"*So, this is Yellow Horse,*" she thought. He really did look like a typical plainsman, right down to the pistol tucked into his belt and the big Bowie knife on his hip. Only the long braids wrapped in buckskin betrayed his native heritage. He was exactly as he'd been described to her. His interest in Lucy was obvious, but his manners were impeccable.

"I'm pleased to meet thee, Mr. Yellow Horse. My husband has mentioned thee. I understand thou are to buy cattle in Texas on behalf of Chief Parker. Will thou be leaving us soon?"

"Tomorrow, Mrs. Jones, I ride for Texas tomorrow.

"So soon..." Lucy said, somewhat too quickly.

Yellow Horse smiled.

"If things go well, I'll be back in about two weeks, give or take a few days."

"Will it be dangerous?" Lucy asked

"Perhaps, but I don't expect we'll have any Indian trouble." He smiled at his own joke.

Lucy blushed, beet red. Mrs. Jones looked startled.

"On the other hand, trail drives are never routine. Cattle can be unpredictable. The country is rough and the weather may change." He added, trying to put the women more at ease.

"How far must thou travel to buy the cattle, Mr. Yellow Horse?"

"I'm not sure, Mrs. Jones. I hope to buy them in the Panhandle. If not, I'll work my way south until I find a seller. I'll have to hire trail hands, put together a remuda for em, and outfit a cook wagon."

"What is a remuda?" Lucy asked.

"It's a string of horses, Miss Meadows. Each man will need at least three. Six would be better."

"My goodness, how many cattle are you buying?"

"It's not about the number of cattle. The horses have a job of work to do keeping the herd together, and moving in the right direction across open country. The men ride all day, at least twelve hours, each and every day. We take turns riding night herd. If a man only changes horses every four hours or so, that's at least three horses per day. Some days, they need four or more. Horses get hurt or go lame. You can't herd wild cattle on foot, Miss Meadows."

"Please, call me Lucy. May I call you James?"

"Thank you, Lucy. I prefer to be called Yellow Horse, but in your case I'll make an exception."

"I see, thank you. I had no idea it was so difficult to herd cattle, James."

"These aren't the family milk cows coming home to be milked. I don't suppose you've ever seen a herd of wild longhorns."

"No, I can't imagine. It must be something to see."

"Most of the major trails cross through the Territory. The Chisholm Trail goes right through this area. Dozens of herds go up it each year, moving tens of thousands of cattle to the railroad. Now that it's spring, they'll be coming. Would you like to ride out and see a big herd sometime, Lucy?"

"Oh, I'd love to James."

"Can you ride a horse?"

"I've never had occasion to ride a horse. Can one purchase a suitable riding habit in the sutler's store? Will you teach me to ride, James?"

The questions made his head swim for a moment. He'd seen a few white women riding horses, but none who rode like a man.

"I believe it's customary for ladies to ride side saddle. Her horse has to be trained to be ridden that way."

"Oh, is that a problem. Can you train the horse for me?"

Yellow Horse restrained the urge to laugh.

"Lucy, that takes some time. I'm bound for Texas, remember?"

"Some of the officer's wives ride, Lucy. Perhaps thee could take lessons with one of them," Alice said.

"Maybe we'll just rent a buggy," Yellow Horse said.

"Is this Indian bothering you, ladies?"

Unnoticed by them, Lieutenant Fitzpatrick had stepped up on the boardwalk and was now standing a few feet away. His angry countenance suggested the reason he was not tipping his hat to the ladies.

"Oh, hello, Lieutenant, no, of course James isn't bothering us. We were just discussing riding out to see one of the big cattle drives coming through the area."

"If that's something you want to do, I can arrange a cavalry escort, and I'll be happy to take you myself."

It took Lucy a moment to realize what was happening.

Yellow Horse recognized it at once.

"If you ladies will excuse me, I have business in the store," he said.

Alice decided to avail herself of the opportunity to leave Lucy in the company of a suitable representative of the army.

"I do as well, may I accompany thee, Mr. Yellow Horse."

Lucy was thunderstruck. How could both her friends abandon her so suddenly?

"OK, I'll be along in a moment," she said to the pair, now going up the steps. She turned her attention back to the dashing young Lieutenant. "Thank you, Lieutenant Fitzpatrick. That is a very thoughtful suggestion."

"It would be my pleasure. I don't think it would be either safe or appropriate for you to go riding off alone with some Indian. I'm quite certain your father would not approve."

"James is perfectly capable of protecting me from harm. I'm told he has considerable experience with large herds of cattle. As for appropriate, that's not your decision to make."

"As may be, I said your *father* would not approve."

Lucy didn't care for his tone.

"It's none of his business."

"I don't think he would see it that way. I suggest you discuss it with him."

"Well, *I* suggest *you* have a nice day. Excuse me, Lieutenant; I'm going to rejoin my friends."

"Yes, of course. Please, Miss Meadows, I intended no offense. I just want you to think of me as a friend. May I call on you?"

"What? Oh…um, yes, I suppose…"

"Excellent," Lieutenant Fitzpatrick said with a grin, tipping his hat. "By the way, my name is George. May I call you Lucy?"

Lucy almost giggled. This was a ridiculous turn of events.

"Yes, George, you may."

"Thank you, Lucy. May I walk you inside?"

She couldn't resist the urge to give him a taste of his own medicine.

"No, thank you, Lieutenant, I don't think it would be safe or appropriate. I'm quite certain my father wouldn't approve. I suggest you discuss it with him."

With that, she turned away, leaving him standing alone. He found himself staring after her with a red face and tight lips.

Watching through a window from inside the store, Yellow Horse couldn't hear what was said, but he saw the resulting expression on the young lieutenant's face. He couldn't stop himself from smiling at the other man's discomfort.

CHAPTER 18

From his position high on the rim of the immense opening in the earth, Yellow Horse sat on his horse and appraised the vast area before him.

For hundreds of years the Palo Duro Canyon was the home range for the Quahadi Comanche. His bond with this canyon was as much spiritual as it was sensory.

This was where he'd been born and where, just two years before, Quanah had made one last stand against the Army of the United States. Now the canyon land, about seventy miles long and averaging five miles wide, was considered the property of the white people, and used as open range. He hadn't been here since the surrender.

Somewhere down there, Charlie Goodnight had a dugout cabin and was running over a thousand head of longhorns.

Yellow Horse was looking for sign.

His keen eyes soon spotted a far off wisp of smoke. Determining distance in this country could be difficult, the terrain was deceiving, but Yellow Horse estimated the smoke originated less than three miles away and no more than six hundred feet lower.

He figured he knew the spot. It would be right beside the Prairie Dog Fork of the Red River. The smoke appeared to be coming from a place his people had camped for as long as they could remember.

He continued studying the canyon as he considered how best to proceed.

Goodnight was a former enemy, a longtime friend and sometimes employer. Unlike many white men, Charlie Goodnight was not a man who judged others by their appearance or ethnic origins. At the same time, he was, like most of the earlier frontiersmen, not a man to cross.

Would he receive Yellow Horse as a friend or see him as a trespasser and recent enemy? They'd been on different sides during the Buffalo War. Even so, Goodnight and he had worked together to secure safety and decent treatment for the Quahadi band of Comanche after the surrender. If it weren't for Goodnight, he would never have driven cattle, met John Everett Sage, or scouted for the Rangers. If he hadn't met Goodnight, he probably wouldn't have lived most of his adult life in the white man's world.

Yellow Horse sat for a time, reflecting on the changes the last few years had brought to his people. He'd known from his youth the white men would not be stopped from coming west, taking the land for themselves.

As a boy, he'd seen their great cities, railroads and steamships. He heard how the great tribes in the east had been driven from their lands. So, after he made his way back to the Comancheria, he'd counseled with the Comanche, Kiowa, Apache, Cheyenne and others, telling them of what he'd seen and the inevitability of what the whites were now calling "manifest destiny". It put his people in an impossible position.

The council fires would burn for days as the choices were discussed. Some bands chose to attempt a peaceful co-existence with the influx of white people, others chose to fight.

Even Quanah had been pushed into a fight he would rather have avoided. When the American government encouraged the mass slaughter of the buffalo, there was no other choice left.

Now it was said only the Sioux to the north, and the Apache to the southwest, continued the fight.

In the winter, <u>Tu-ukumah</u> had taken his men and left the reservation. Now, somewhere out on the Llano Estacado, he was raiding the buffalo hunters with less than two hundred Comanche beside him.

Yellow Horse bowed his head, as he considered the outcome for those last, fierce warriors. Their days were now numbered. If any survived, they would live as prisoners of the American government.

It seemed like only yesterday his people roamed free, following the buffalo across the prairie. They'd had a fine camp, right here in Palo Duro Canyon.

As he thought about that, he remembered Quanah's admonition. Yes, he lived among the whites, but in his heart he was not yet at peace. How could he be? It was true; he was sickened by the way the times were changing.

Nearly every day he was subjected to new examples of the white man's abuses. There was a smoldering resentment at the core of his being. He fought against it, even as he drew energy from it. Some days he was close to surrendering to his anger and striking out against the usurpers who had taken so much from his people. He longed for a day when the Comanche would drive out the whites and once again be rulers of the plains, a day he knew could never come.

Yellow Horse shook his head.

This was not a healthy way to think. Like Quanah, he too must find a way to live in peace. Quanah spoke of Christianity as a way of peace. Was that the source from which Quanah had found his way?

After a moment he took a deep breath and straightened up, tall in the saddle. It would do no good to dwell on the past. Those days were gone forever. Tomorrow was only a dream. Today he had work to do.

***

"Rider coming in," Pancho called.

Charlie Goodnight stood up and stretched, letting the freshly branded calf go back to his mamma. He studied the approaching horseman.

"Comanche, looks like…Well I'll be—it's Yellow Horse. I heard he was off scouting for the Rangers."

Pancho squinted at the distant rider. Not for the first time wondering, at this distance, how was Goodnight able to see all that? To Poncho, the rider appeared to be a man on a white horse, probably a cowboy. Other than that, he had no clue.

"How can you tell, Senõr Goodnight?

"…The way he sits his horse and carries his rifle."

"How do you want to handle this, Mr. Goodnight?" One of the hands asked.

"Let's start by offering him some coffee. I expect we'll be palavering for a spell. Here, Glenn, take over for me. There're plenty more calves to brand"

"Mr. Adair will be along any time now."

"Don't matter. Yellow Horse wouldn't come here to waste my time. You've got work to do. Now get to it."

When Yellow Horse rode up, he found Charlie Goodnight at the edge of the herd waiting for him by the chuck wagon.

"…Mornin', Charlie."

"…Same to you, Yellow Horse. Step down and we'll drink some coffee."

"Obliged."

When they were seated on canvas chairs in the shade of the chuck wagon, Goodnight spoke up.

"What brings you back this way, my friend?"

"Business, Quanah wants to buy cattle."

"Quanah used to steal my cattle. Now he wants to buy them?"

"He does."

"OK. If he has money, I've got the beef. Will they let him run cattle on the reservation?"

"Yep, they say it's our land to use as we see fit. We got permission from the Agency and the Army."

Goodnight nodded thoughtfully.

"…How many head?"

"One hundred and seventy five heifers or young cows, and twenty five bulls or bull calves. At least five must be mature bulls."

"No steers?"

"No."

"Sounds like Quanah's planning to start a cow/calf operation."

Yellow Horse shrugged.

"Among other things."

"You his agent?"

"I am."

Just then, Pancho jogged up to the chuck wagon.

"Senõr Adair's herd and wagons are coming in.

"Bueno."

"What should we do?"

"Run his herd into the pens over against the canyon wall. He can park his wagons wherever he wants to."

"He'll want to see you."

"I'll be along directly, or hang on, just send him over here. I'm doing business with Yellow Horse. He can come over here."

Pancho looked back and forth between the two men.

"Si, Jefe."

As though they hadn't been interrupted, Charlie Goodnight picked up the conversation right where they'd left off.

"As Quanah's agent, I expect you'll want to select the stock."

"I will."

"…Fair enough. How soon do you want to do it?"

"You say when."

"We need to settle the price. What do you say to fifteen dollars a head, where they stand?"

"Done."

"You want some of my drovers to deliver em to Fort Sill?"

"Yes."

"Men and horses don't come cheap. That'll cost Quanah an extra three dollars per head."

"One dollar a head."

"Two dollars, and I'll provide the cook and the chuck wagon."

"Fifty cents and I ramrod the outfit. The drovers answer to me."

Goodnight chuckled.

"Quanah Parker picked the right man for the job. It figures, don't it? It's what I get for training you myself. You won't budge, will you, Yellow Horse? OK then, seventeen dollars per head, delivered to Fort Sill. Let's call it done."

"Sixteen dollars, do we have a deal?"

The two men were shaking hands when John Adair arrived at the chuck wagon.

"I say, Charles. I expected a better welcome... Hello, who do we have here?"

"John Adair, meet James Yellow Horse."

"Good heavens. I believe you told me something about this fellow on a previous occasion. A red Indian, if I'm not mistaken. By the looks of him, he could pass for a white man. You will understand my surprise. What marvelous grey eyes he has."

"Yellow Horse is a cattle buyer from Fort Sill."

"Is he? Well, I hope you told him my cattle are not for sale."

Yellow Horse squinted at the man who spoke of him as though he wasn't standing right there.

Seeing this, Goodnight made the introductions.

"Yellow Horse, meet John Adair. Mr. Adair comes from England, though lately he's been a financier in Denver. We're going to start a ranch together. We brought a hundred head of Durham cattle down from Colorado. He thinks highly of the breed."

"Howdy." Yellow Horse said, extending his hand.

"Good day to you, sir. May I call you James?"

"No."

"I say, what a rude fellow. I've offered my hand in friendship...Oh well, as you like."

"Easy now, John, Yellow Horse ain't rude. He just don't like the name, James."

"Ahh, I see. So, is it Jim, then? Perhaps, Jimmy. Which do you prefer?"

"Yellow Horse."

"You do not use your Christian name?"

"No. I'm not what you'd call a Christian."

"What? Oh, I see. My word, what an interesting notion, I must say."

Yellow Horse turned back to Goodnight.

"When can I select the stock?"

"Tomorrow. I'll have three or four hundred head pushed into a side canyon. You can look um over and mark the one's you want.

We'll cut the others out and hold your stock together. I'll put together some good hands and a remuda. So, you can hit the trail day after tomorrow. Will that do?"

Yellow Horse nodded.

"That'll do. I saw buffalo tracks a couple miles east of here. They were drifting towards the Spanish Skirts."

"Yep. There's still a small herd here in the canyon. I'll see they don't get hunted."

"Appreciate it."

Goodnight returned a slight nod of his head.

John Adair spoke up.

"Listen, Mr. Yellow Horse. This country abounds with the scruffy Longhorn and little else. I doubt you have had occasion to examine quality cattle. Perhaps you would enjoy looking over my herd of Durham shorthorns. They are the finest cattle ever seen on this continent."

Yellow Horse looked at Charlie Goodnight.

Goodnight sighed and said, "I want to look um over myself. After the drive down from Colorado, I'm curious to see what kinda shape they're in. Alright, John, show us the stock. I expect now's as good a time as any."

CHAPTER 14

"Good evening, Colonel, Miss Meadows." Lieutenant Fitzpatrick said as he approached the porch, removing his hat.

"Good evening, George. We're off duty, there's no need for formalities."

"Thank you, sir. Lucy, I've spoken to your father, and he's given me permission to call on you."

"Has he? I already told you it would be fine with me."

"Yes, ma'am, but I thought it appropriate to ask him."

"You seem awfully fond of the word 'appropriate', Lieutenant." Lucy said, with a sniff.

"If you young people will excuse me, I think I'll go inside and read for a while. Here, George, take my seat."

"Thank you, sir."

After the Colonel retired for the evening, the two sat in silence. Lieutenant Fitzpatrick continued holding his hat in his lap. Lucy became annoyed.

"Tell me, George, what do you do for fun around here?"

"Fun? Well, there's usually a pretty good poker game at the infirmary on Friday nights."

"Charming, I'm sure."

"Oh, right. I see what you mean. What sort of things did you do for fun—back east?"

"We went boating, to cotillions, soirees, concerts, dining out, picnics in the park, lots of things."

"Yes, I remember those things. It seems far away and long ago, now."

"Oh please, George, you're not that old."

"No, I was just thinking how my life has changed since those days. We do have parties, balls, and holiday celebrations here at the fort. They tend to be somewhat formal affairs."

"Well, there's nothing wrong with that. I've never asked. Where are you from, George?"

"Pennsylvania, Philadelphia to be more precise."

"Oh my, you are a long way from home."

"Yes, but home for me is wherever I'm stationed."

"How long have you been in the army?"

"It'll be two years, come September, but I was four years at West Point."

"You don't seem that much older than me. How old are you?"

"I'm twenty three, Lucy. How old are you?"

"That is not the sort of question a gentleman asks a lady"

"Indeed. I beg your pardon."

"Not at all, you're only a couple of years older. Tell me, why did you join the army?"

"It's funny how just a couple of year's difference in age can have such a dramatic effect on our perceptions. I guess I joined because my older brother did. I decided to become an officer. I wanted to do everything he did."

"Have you?"

Lieutenant Fitzpatrick looked at Lucy. What she saw in his eyes was a depth and sadness she didn't know he was capable of.

"All but one thing, he was killed in the second battle of Bull Run."

"Oh, George, I'm so sorry." She reached out to touch his arm.

"He was ten years older than me, and I worshipped him. I was determined to follow in his footsteps. My family name had some influence, and I was a high achiever in school. I was granted an appointment to West Point. After graduation and my commission, I was sent west, most recently here, to Fort Sill. I haven't been back to Philadelphia since I was eighteen years old."

"How does your family feel about that?"

"I have no family. My father died shortly after I was born. I guess that's why my older brother was my hero. My mother died just before I left for West Point. There's nothing for me back east. This is my life now."

"What do you enjoy most about life on a frontier outpost?"

"It's the country, Lucy. This continent is two thousand miles wide, coast to coast. I've seen some of the west, and it's amazing.

You should see the Rocky Mountains in the springtime. You can't imagine. If you think it's beautiful here, you should see that."

"I don't think it *is* beautiful here. I think it's dismal, barren and harsh."

"No, it's nothing like that. You're talking about the desert. I've been in the desert. Even the desert can be beautiful."

"Really, there's somewhere more barren and harsh than this part of the country?"

George laughed. Lucy found his mirth annoying and yet somehow appealing.

"Yes, Lucy. The desert is both harsh and beautiful. It seems almost totally barren, even the ground seems to be nothing but hardpan, but it's actually teeming with life."

"I thought the definition of a desert was a scarcity of water. Don't people die of thirst in the desert?"

"Sure, I said it was harsh. It's not an easy place to stay alive, but it's still beautiful. Not as beautiful as you, but…"

"What a nice compliment, George. Thank you. Do you really think I'm beautiful?"

"Yes, I do."

"You're just saying that, but it's very sweet of you."

"No, I mean it. You're as pretty as a desert rose."

They passed the next hour in a more amiable manner.

CHAPTER 15

When Yellow Horse rode up to the fire where Charlie Goodnight and John Adair were drinking their first cup of coffee, the morning sky was just beginning to turn pink. It would be nearly another thirty minutes before the sun would rise above the canyon rim.

"Mornin', Yellow Horse. I figured you'd want to get an early start. We're fixin' to eat breakfast. Step down and join us." Charlie Goodnight said.

Yellow Horse smiled and nodded.

"Obliged."

After securing his horse he joined the men at the fire. The cook poured him a cup of coffee.

"I say, Mr. Yellow Horse. Charles tells me you are acting as agent for the great Comanche war chief, Quanah Parker. I would be honored to present him with the gift of four young Durham bulls, of your choosing."

Yellow Horse was stunned. Why would a white man give such a valuable gift to an Indian? It put him in a difficult position.

"That's very generous, Mr. Adair. I'm sure Quanah will be pleased. I hesitate to accept. It's a custom among my people, when someone gives you a gift; you give a gift in return. I'm at a loss. We didn't anticipate your kindness."

"Think nothing of it, old man. I'm delighted to do it. I know the quality of Chief Parker's herd will be greatly improved."

"Yes, sir, I'm sure it will be. Still, I'm obliged to offer a gift in return."

Yellow Horse walked over to where his horse was tied. He removed the rifle from the scabbard on his saddle and returned to the edge of the fire.

"Other than my horse, this is the only thing I have of any value. Please accept this rifle as a token of Quanah's appreciation."

"What, what? I say, I can't imagine a more marvelous gift."

John Adair whistled as he examined the rifle.

"By Jove, will you look at that? This is a Henry rifle, is it not?"

Yellow Horse nodded.

"You've put brass studs in the buttstock, by way of customizing it. Is that an eagle feather hanging down there?"

Another silent nod affirmed the statement.

"Imagine that. I own a rifle once carried in battle by a Comanche Indian. I'll bet you've killed white men with this rifle."

Yellow Horse stiffened, glancing at Charlie Goodnight who'd been watching this exchange with some interest. Goodnight spoke up.

"No, John. Yellow Horse bought that rifle last year, at a store in Fort Worth."

"Oh? Well, that is disappointing. Still, it's a fine gift, and I thank you for it."

"Charlie, I'd like to get started choosing the cattle." Yellow Horse said, changing the subject.

"Can't a man eat his breakfast? My boys won't have those critters boxed up till later this morning." Goodnight said.

Catching the hint, the cook began loading up the plates with bacon, beans and biscuits.

Yellow Horse shrugged, accepting the plate Goodnight offered him. John Adair wandered away to store the rifle in his wagon.

"It ain't like you to speak lies, Charlie. You know I've had that rifle since before we met. That's been more than a dozen years back. I've used it in several fights."

"Yeah, well—he don't need to know all that." Goodnight said, with a wink. "Still, I'm surprised. A Comanche doesn't give his rifle to an enemy."

"I had it to do. Besides, he is not my enemy."

Goodnight shrugged and changed the subject again.

"I've got a crew for you. You'll know a couple of the hands from drives you made together some time back. When I told the men you were going to ramrod the outfit, why, they volunteered to ride with you."

"Good…and the rest?"

"They're youngsters, mostly. Only a few of um, never been on a drive before."

"Charlie…"

"Now, don't worry, Yellow Horse. They're all good hands. They just ain't been up the trail, yet. A short drive like this will be a good way to break em in. What do you expect for two dollars a head?"

Shaking his head, Yellow Horse looked at Goodnight, held up one finger, and growled.

DAN ARNOLD

CHAPTER 16

Yellow Horse spent the day selecting stock and helping sort them out from the more than four hundred head being held in a side canyon.

John Adair was true to his word, sending four young Durham bulls to join the two hundred head herd now ready for the drive to Fort Sill.

At supper time, Yellow Horse and Goodnight met with seven other men to discuss the drive.

Charles Goodnight looked around at the cowboys gathered around the fire.

"Boys, this is Yellow Horse. We've moved many a herd up the trail together. He's as good a hand as I know. I'd like to have him back with me now, but I reckon that train has left the station. He's the ramrod for the drive into the Indian Territory. You follow his orders, same as if he were me.

Yellow Horse, I expect you know some of these men. Is there anything you want to say?"

Yellow Horse recognized men he'd worked with before. Seldon Lindsey, John Reynolds Hughes, and the wrangler, "Shorty" Parmenter, were all good hands who'd been with him on previous drives. He was thankful Goodnight wasn't saddling him with nothing but green hands and tenderfeet.

The other four men, including three youngsters and the cook, were new faces. He figured he should say something for their benefit.

"Thanks, Charlie. Here's what y'all need to know. Shorty will show you which horses are in your string. Be ready to ride at first light. You'll be plenty busy tomorrow, and every day from here on. Holding the herd together and keeping them moving will be tough work. Right off, there'll be bunch quitters trying to turn back for the home range. When your horse starts to tire, get another. Figure on long days in the saddle and too little sleep at night.

I scouted the trail on my way here. We'll have plenty of water, but the spring grass is just greening up. That means we'll have to give the herd more time to graze in the evenings.

This is a short drive. We could get it done in three or four days and get there gaunt, or do it in five or six days, and bring in a better herd. We'll take our time.

Even though it is a short drive, there'll still be all the usual perils along the way. The biggest threat is weather. Thunder and lightning can stampede a herd, and at this time of year we can expect to get caught in a thunderstorm. If it happens, it's better in daylight than after dark.

YELLOW HORSE

The country is rough and there are streams to cross. Another thing, I've seen sign of riders above the canyon. I expect there're rustlers in the area. To them, a small herd like this is easy pickin's. So, be ready.

For you men who've done his before, it's business as usual. For the rest of you; understand this—my job is to bring in the herd in the best shape possible. The same goes for y'all. I don't figure to lose even one of you. That said, look to your own safety. These are wild longhorns in open country. A careless moment or one mistake could cost you your life.

I won't tolerate drinking or fighting. You want to do either one, wait till you get to civilization. Do what I tell you, when I tell you, and we'll get along fine. If you cross me, I'll gut you…any questions?"

The new cowboys stiffened a bit when they heard that last comment. The men who knew Yellow Horse didn't turn a hair. They'd been expecting a similar statement, and they knew he meant it.

***

The drive started with as much difficulty as expected. Down in the canyon the herd wanted to split up and return to the other cattle. When they topped out on the plains, they tried to scatter. The green riders had to be told what to do, and watched to make sure they did it right. They were on the trail for more than eight hours before the herd began to settle into a steady stream behind the leaders.

When it looked like things were under control, Yellow Horse rode ahead to locate a good spot to rest the herd for the night. He'd left instructions with the point riders to push the cattle southeast toward Flat Turtle Creek.

As he approached the creek, he saw fresh horse tracks, a lot of them. Dismounting, he examined the tracks and determined they were not made by a cavalry patrol. Seven riders in a ragged group had ridden slowly through here on a northwest course before suddenly breaking into a trot and veering due north.

Although they were headed in the same general direction from which he'd just come, he hadn't seen them as he approached. Were they keeping watch and seeing him in the distance, turned away to avoid contact?

There could be many reasons a group of riders were out in the middle of nowhere. Maybe it was a company of buffalo hunters. It could be a posse in pursuit of an outlaw. It might even be some cowboys searching for wild or stray cattle. These appeared to be the tracks of the same men he'd seen near the edge of the canyon just a couple of days back.

While nothing in the tracks told him who the riders were, he had a bad feeling.

Looking up at the sky, Yellow Horse sighed.

He wanted to know for sure and certain why seven mounted men were traveling so close to his herd. He figured he already knew. He hoped he was wrong.

Either way, he had things to do. The first thing, find a place to rest the cattle, horses and men. The second was to ride back to the herd and lead them to the bedding ground.

About a quarter of a mile downstream, around a bend in the creek, he found an open meadow on nearly level ground between two low, brush covered hills. The creek flowed along one side, and mesquite thickets dotted with prickly pear defined the surrounding edges. This would be as good a place as any to hold the herd overnight.

In the morning they would push across the creek and continue southeast.

Yellow Horse twisted his head, trying to ease a crick out of his neck.

He wondered if they would still have a herd, when the sun came up.

DAN ARNOLD

CHAPTER 17

"Thou seem preoccupied, Lucy. Are thou feeling unwell?"

"What? No, Alice, I'm fine. I guess I *am* a little preoccupied. Lieutenant Fitzpatrick came calling the other evening."

"Perhaps thou should consider it a compliment."

"Oh, I do. It's just confusing. I haven't seen him since then."

"Did thee say or do something to offend him?"

"No. I'm sure he'll come calling again. That's not what's confusing me."

"Is there something I can do to help thee?"

"You're a married woman. How did you know Lee would be the right man for you?"

Alice Jones smiled, patting Lucy's hand.

"Aren't thee getting a little ahead of thy self?"

Lucy smiled back.

"I'm just curious. How did you know?"

Alice was thoughtful for a moment.

"I knew what I would require of a man. I needed a man who would love me, and always be there for me, the sort of man who could be a good father to our children. Naturally, being a woman, I wanted a strong handsome man to come sweep me off my feet."

Lucy was surprised. She didn't consider Lee Jones to be all that good looking.

"Did Lee do that?"

"No. He won my heart."

"How, I mean, what did he do?"

"I'm not sure it was anything he did. I think God may have done something in me."

"I don't understand."

"Lucy, it's only natural thee are curious. Thee have thoughts and feelings about what marriage might be like. I did too. I had romantic notions about a knight in shining armor that would treat me like a queen."

Lucy nodded her encouragement.

"Marriage is nothing like what I imagined. It's difficult. It's wonderful and horrible, all on the same day. The idea that there is some perfect man out there just waiting for thee is vain and foolish. There is no perfect man, and we are not perfect women."

"That doesn't answer my question. How did you know Lee would be the right man for you?"

"I didn't. I trusted God. I knew I needed a Christian man who would share my beliefs and be a leader in our home. Lee is that kind of man. He isn't the man I dreamed of. He's the man God provided, and that makes him better than I could've dreamed of. Does this make sense to thee?"

Lucy was thoughtful.

"I think so. What you're saying is I should trust that God will provide the right man."

"Not exactly, I think I'm trying to say God can make a good man, the right man for thee."

"That doesn't really help. It sounds like you're telling me it's up to me to pick one, and hope God will make him better."

Alice shrugged. She was having a hard time trying to answer the question.

Lucy sighed.

"I don't think God is in the business of turning toads into princes."

"Must thee choose from a list of toads?"

Lucy laughed.

"No, well, not exactly."

"Are thee thinking Lieutenant Fitzpatrick might be a toad?"

"No, he's charming really, in a very reserved sort of way. He's just so stiff and proper."

"Is there someone thee finds more appealing?"

"I don't know…"

"Is Lieutenant Fitzpatrick interested in thee?"

"Well, yes, he's certainly interested in me, but Yellow Horse is more interesting *to* me."

Alice frowned. How could she tell Lucy it would be unacceptable in polite society for a white woman to marry an Indian? Life was already hard enough without taking on such a terrible burden. She knew Lucy well enough not to try telling her so. Lucy might well do the opposite of what she was told.

"Thou should bring these things to God in prayer."

"I know, and I do. I just don't know what I should do."

"Try to be patient, my friend. These things cannot be hurried."

"I just wish Yellow Horse would come back from Texas."

"Perhaps there is a reason he hasn't. God's timing is always perfect."

Lucy frowned, tapping her foot.

"Yes, but I'm confused *now*."

"Lucy, are thee considering Yellow Horse as a serious marriage prospect?"

"No, well, maybe. Why do you ask?"

"He belongs to a different culture. He hasn't taken a wife among his own people. He is a man who likes to roam. Do thou think he would, or could, settle down with thee?"

"That's a good question. I'll bet he would for the right woman."

"He is a man shaped by this wild country, Lucy. I fear he has no desire to become more civilized."

"Well, I'll bet I could tame him. He already lives in our culture, and he's more sophisticated than many white men. I'd have him eating out of my hand in no time."

"No. Thou mustn't think that way. Even if thou could, would thou want to change him from what he is now?"

"No, I suppose not. It's part of what I find so intriguing about him."

"Believe me, Lucy. A woman cannot make a man into anything she wants him to be."

"I could change. I could be whatever he needs me to be."

Alice looked away, gathering her thoughts.

"Lucy, thou shouldn't have to change for any man. A man, who loves thee, loves thee just as thou are."

"Oh fiddle. I don't know what to do."

Alice took her friend's hands into her own.

"There is no hurry, Lucy. I'm delighted to be thy friend. Thou can talk with me about such things anytime thee wants."

"I know, Alice. Thank you. I suppose some things just need to be lived. Most women my age are married. I've had a few beaus, but I became bored with them pretty quickly. They seem more interested in their careers than they are in me. George strikes me as that sort of man. I've never met a man quite like Yellow Horse."

"No, very few people have."

DAN ARNOLD

CHAPTER 18

Yellow Horse looked at the men gathered around the cook fire. "Y'all listen up, there's something you should know. We're about to be attacked by a gang of outlaws."

The startled reaction of the men didn't surprise him. This was only the first night of the drive. He didn't mince words.

"They'll plan to hit us in the hours just before dawn. That's when we'd be in our deepest sleep, and the nighthawks least alert. They'll come in fast, scattering the horse herd, shooting the nighthawks, and anyone else they can get a shot at.

Once they stampede the herd they'll drift along with the biggest bunch, till they settle down. Then, they'll round up all they can, and take what they have to Kansas or New Mexico. They might not get the whole herd, but they'll get enough. They'll leave behind a wrecked camp, scattered strays and dead men. I don't figure to let that happen."

"What makes you so sure there're rustlers out there somewhere?" The cook, Dusty Wharton, asked.

"I've seen the sign. After we got the herd settled, I picked up their trail and tracked em. There are seven men camped on the other side of that hill behind me. They may be watching us right now. I can't think of another reason they'd be out there."

"How do you want to handle it?" Seldon Lindsey asked.

"I don't intend to wait for them to hit us. I mean to jump them in their camp after it gets dark. Who'll go with me?"

There was silence for a moment as the men considered the plan.

"I'll go." John Hughes said.

"I'm in." Seldon Lindsey volunteered.

"I don't cotton to waiting for somebody to try to kill me, or letting Mr. Goodnight's remuda get run off. So, I'm in too." Shorty Parmenter said.

"I reckon we'll all go." Dusty Wharton added.

"No, I need some of you to stay with the herd. I want four men riding nighthawk. Those two boys out there now need to be told what's happening, and what to do if we can't stop the rustlers.

Toby, I need you and Shorty to ride out there. Tell Stan and George to be extra alert. The four of y'all spread out about an equal distance apart. If they hit the herd, don't try to stop them. I don't want anyone shot or trampled in a stampede. If men come at you shooting, take off. If the herd jumps up, slap spurs to your pony, and run like a cat with his tail on fire. We can round up stray cattle later. Having to bury what's left of you, would slow us down. Do you understand, Toby?"

"Yes sir, Mr. Yellow Horse."

"A while after you get to the herd you may hear some shooting off in the distance. Don't worry about it. Just keep an eye on the cattle…any questions?"

"What should we do if you don't come back?" The youngster asked.

Yellow Horse grinned.

"Keep moving the herd southeast. In four or five days, you'll cross the river into the Indian Nations. Sooner or later, you'll come across someone who can give you directions to Quanah Parkers camp. Deliver the herd and collect your pay. That's what you signed on for, ain't it, Toby?"

"We'll get it done."

"I know you will. Don't worry. We'll be back. I doubt you'll even lose much sleep. Just stay sharp and watchful. If you see someone coming along quiet like, don't panic or start shooting. Chances are it'll be the four of us coming to relieve you."

"I sure hope so."

Yellow Horse glanced at Shorty, who nodded and winked.

"Come on, Toby, let's mount up and ride out to the herd," he said.

As the four men watched the two cowboys riding away from camp, Dusty Wharton turned to Yellow Horse and asked,

"You won't mind if I bring my scattergun, will you?"

"Nope, we might need it."

"What's the plan?"

"As soon as it gets dark, we'll make it look like we're bedding down for the night. We'll leave the lanterns lit and stoke the fire. One by one, we'll slip off into the mesquite and meet by the side of the creek."

"Then what?" Seldon Lindsey asked.

"I know where they're camped. We'll work our way up the draw and around the hill. If they have a sentry, he'll be at the top of the hill. I'll deal with him. While I'm doing that, y'all spread out around the edge of their campsite.

Wait for me. I mean to parley, see if we can avoid a fight. They'll probably have their horses picketed, ready to ride. While I'm talking, if one of you gets the chance, ease up among em and set em loose. If the parley don't work, and I move sudden like, open up on the rustlers and kill every one of them. That's it, and that's all."

***

Six men were sitting by a single small campfire, passing a bottle of whisky around.

"Hello, the camp." Yellow Horse called.

The men around the fire jumped to their feet, guns in hand.

"Hello yourself, who goes there?"

"My name is James. I saw your fire. I'm alone and on foot. I sure could use some coffee. Can I come in?"

"OK, Mr. James, come on in, but keep your hands where we can see em."

"Much obliged. Say, you boys are kinda jumpy. Are there Indians about?"

With his hair tucked up into his hat, Yellow Horse looked like any white man. He walked into the light of the fire with his hands raised in front of him.

"Injuns? You never know. Better safe than sorry. You just startled us, is all."

"I apologize. Being on foot, I don't make much noise. That coffee smells good. Can I get a cup?"

"Help yourself. What are you doing out here on foot?"

As he squatted by the fire, Yellow Horse scanned the six men around him. He poured coffee into a tin cup, holding it in his left hand. The men began to relax, holstering their pistols, but still wary of the stranger in their midst. He stood and took a step back from the fire.

"I got into a little shooting scrape some miles east of here. My horse went down. I was lucky to get away."

"Get away from what?" The apparent leader of the group asked.

"Trouble, I think it best to avoid trouble. Wouldn't you agree?"

"I reckon trouble comes to us all," the leader of the gang said.

"It surely does. I try to avoid it, but it still comes around. Say, aren't you Joe Murdock?"

"What's it to you. I don't believe I know you, Mr. James."

"No sir, we've never met. I saw your picture once, and read about you in the newspapers. You're a famous outlaw. Listen, Mr. Murdock, I'm down on my luck. If you need another man…"

"…Another man for what?"

"It don't matter to me. I'll do anything you need me to."

"Are you on the dodge?"

"You could say that."

Joe Murdock looked around at the other men. They showed no sign, one way or the other. He took a moment to consider his answer.

"Another man means another mouth to feed, and less profit for the rest of us. On the other hand, if you're any good, you might earn your groceries. Are you any good?"

"I can take care of myself. I'll work as hard as any man, and I ain't particular about what I do."

"Can you shoot?"

"I hit what I aim at."

"Can you shoot a man?"

Yellow Horse nodded.

"I have."

"You any good with cattle?"

"…Better than most. I've been up the trail."

"I got no use for a man without a horse. We don't have extras, but I know where you can get one."

"Where's that?"

"Less than a mile from here, there's a trail herd. You could sneak down there and steal one of theirs."

"Where's the herd?"

"Their camp is down around the other side of this hill. We're going to pay them a visit in a few hours. You ease on down there and wait for us. When the shooting starts, get you a horse, any way you can. You won't have much warning or much time. The cattle will stampede and we're going with em. We'll see if you're any good."

"How many men do they have?"

"Eight. Why do you ask?"

"There're only six of you."

"Seven. We've got a lookout up on the top of the hill. If you're with us that makes eight."

"What if they know you're coming and they're waiting for you?"

"That would be a problem. "Why, you planning to tell em?"

"Me? No, I'm here to tell you."

"Tell me what?"

"There are only six of you, and you're surrounded. Make the slightest move, and we'll cut you down where you stand."

Joe Murdock's mouth dropped open.

"What? Why?"

"That's my herd down there. I decided to give you one chance to stay alive. This is it. Think about it. A smart choice keeps you alive. Do something stupid, my men shoot you down."

"You're bluffing."

Yellow Horse stood ready, his gun hand casually hovering near the Colt revolver tucked into his belt. The other hand still held the cup of coffee.

"Try me, Murdock. You'll be the first one to die."

"Boss, the horses, somebody turned em loose."

Murdock glanced at the picket line. The horses were wandering away into the night. His mouth formed a thin line as he turned back to the man who called himself "James".

"It's your choice, Murdock. What'll it be?"

"How do you see this playing out?"

"That's up to you. My way, we take your guns and leave you here, alive."

"What makes you think we won't come after you?"

"You're smarter than that. It would be a mighty costly undertaking. Most or all of you would die. Decide right now. Do we fight?"

After a brief pause, Murdock shook his head.

"Not today. I expect we'll meet again, another time, another place."

"Smart move. Now, y'all slowly drop your guns, right where you are. Some of my men will pick them up."

After the guns were gathered, Yellow Horse had the outlaws sit on the ground, spread out, well away from the fire. He, John Hughes, and Dusty Wharton held the men at gunpoint while Seldon Lindsey set out to catch four of the recently freed horses.

Once he and the three cowboys were mounted on the outlaw's horses, Yellow Horse took off his hat. Shaking out his long hair, he addressed the men where they sat.

"My name is Yellow Horse. I don't need to tell you this is dangerous country. Even though you deserve it, I won't set y'all on foot. There're three horses out there somewhere nearby. I expect you can catch em. You'll have to ride double, but it beats walking. I left a rifle next to the body of the man you had up on the hill. If you're careful, you won't starve before you make it somewhere civilized. Stay clear of my herd. If I ever see any of you again, I'll shoot you on sight."

"You must think you're a real generous man." Murdock said.

"I figure I'm more generous to you than you would've been to us. Like I said, my name is Yellow Horse. If you want to find me, ask around. Buenos suerte, y adios."

DAN ARNOLD

CHAPTER 19

Lucy was learning who people were and what they did on the fort.

In addition to Lieutenant Fitzpatrick, she came to know the noncommissioned officers.

The Sergeant Major was the regiment's highest ranking noncommissioned officer. He was also the darkest complexioned man she'd ever met. He'd appointed himself as her chief advisor and protector.

She was also acquainted with the hospital surgeon and steward. She was even on a first name basis with the chief bugler, Corporal Watkins.

The cavalry at Fort Sill also had specialized duty officers, such as the veterinary surgeon, veterinary sergeants, saddlers and farriers.

During the day the sutler's store was the fort's social center. Here, Indians, soldiers, scouts, hunters and travelers passing through, mingled together as they purchased supplies, mailed letters or ordered from catalogues. Anything the army didn't provide could be bought there. Tobacco, coffee, sugar, liquor, and other commodities not otherwise available nearby, were always stocked.

The sutler's store was the best place to learn what was happening in the world outside the fort. In the evenings it was also the bar for the enlisted men. At night, the store would not be a proper place for ladies to appear. She'd been ordered by her father to avoid the place after hours.

Late one afternoon, about a week after Yellow Horse left for Texas, a Tonkawa scout galloped past her on a lathered horse. He reported directly to Captain Lee.

His arrival caused a stir. The routine activities at the fort were disrupted as orders were given and men rushed to obey.

Lucy wrung her hands and paced as she waited for her father to come home.

He didn't arrive at the usual time but some thirty minutes later. When he did, she met him at the door.

She tried to remain calm, but her concern overcame her composure. She searched her father's face. Seeing something like grim resolve in his eyes, she found herself blurting out the question that had been plaguing her for more than an hour.

"What's going on?"

"What do you mean?"

"Something's happening. All of a sudden this place has become a beehive of activity. Are we in danger?"

"No, Lucy. No more than usual. Let me explain. At the end of last year, the war chief Tu-ukumah, and about two hundred renegades, left the reservation with the intent to continue attacks on the buffalo hunters. We attempted to capture them, but lost them in a snow storm. Now we know where they are. It seems your friend Yellow Horse gave us some good information. Tomorrow, the 10th is deploying in pursuit. We should only be in the field a couple of weeks."

"Oh, Daddy, will it be dangerous?"

"I don't believe so. His people have endured a hard winter and they've just been in a fight with buffalo hunters. They're probably suffering. I expect they'll be plenty willing to surrender. It's more of a rescue mission than a military action. This isn't anything for you to worry about."

"Where are you going?"

"Across the Llano Estacado."

"What is that?"

"It's high plains, a barren stretch of ground in north Texas and New Mexico."

"Is it far from here?"

Her father chuckled.

"Baby girl, everything, everywhere, is far from *here*."

Lucy laughed and replied, "So I've noticed."

Her father's face changed.

"Lucy, listen. About that…I love having you here, but this is no place for a young lady of your class. I've written your Aunt Lucille in Baltimore. She would be delighted to have you join her there. She wants to introduce you in society."

"No, I don't want to go."

"This isn't a request. It's an order. I've arranged transportation for you to Dodge City, Kansas. There, you will board the train and go back to Baltimore."

Lucy was furious. She had no intention of being shipped off like a piece of freight.

"How long have you been planning this?"

"Before you arrived, I started looking into where you might go after your visit here. Now that I have to deploy, it's time for you to go. I can't leave you alone here in this place."

"When is this relocation supposed to happen?"

"Tomorrow, after the regiment takes to the field. I've arranged an escort for you under the command of Sergeant Major Jackson. He'll see you board the stage and his troopers will accompany you all the way to Dodge City."

Lucy broke down in tears.

"Daddy, please don't do this. I want to stay. I can be a help to you. I'll keep your house and entertain your guests. Please don't send me away."

"I'm sorry, Lucy. There's no future for you here. This is no life for a well-educated young woman. In Baltimore you'll have opportunity to meet suitors and make a normal healthy home."

"I can do that here."

"You'll end up an Army wife, a widow, or worse. I don't want that for you.

"What about what I want?"

"You don't know what you want. One day you're enamored with Lieutenant Fitzpatrick. The next day you're pining away for the return of Yellow Horse. You've shown far too much interest in that Indian."

So that was it. Lucy was stunned. She didn't know what to say.

"It's just too wild and dangerous here." Her father tried to change the course of the conversation.

Lucy whirled away and rushed into her room, slamming the door behind her.

***

The next morning Lucy awoke to the usual sound of reveille. Her father was already dressed and gone by the time she came out of her room. From the safety of her father's house in the officer's quarters she watched as the troopers assembled.

A little later, a bitterly cold wind greeted her as she joined the other women, wrapped in coats and shawls, standing huddled together on the edge of the parade grounds, watching and waiting to say goodbye to their husbands, sons, and loved ones.

Promptly at nine o'clock; her father, mounted on a fine black horse, appeared on the parade grounds in front of the assembled soldiers. He called out orders. These were repeated by lesser officers. Then, he and Captain Lee turned and rode out onto the road, side by side.

As they fell in behind them, the officers and troopers rode out in a continuous column of four, grouped by company and troop, nearly three hundred men in all. Lieutenant Fitzpatrick placed his hat over his heart as he rode past Lucy.

With the flags and banners snapping in the wind, horses snorting and the band playing, it made quite a spectacle.

There were only four white officers in the regiment. The rest of the 10th Cavalry was entirely made up of black soldiers and non-commissioned officers. Her father had told her, the famed "buffalo soldiers" of the 10th Cavalry Regiment had earned distinction as being among the finest cavalry units ever fielded in combat.

Near the end of the column, supply wagons, light artillery, and the hospital wagon reminded everyone of what was at stake.

As the last of the soldiers rode away, Lucy knew Sergeant Major Jackson would soon be looking for her. She said her good byes to the other ladies and hurried away. She had only a short time to carry out her plan.

CHAPTER 20

Her plan to walk right past the sentries wrapped in a blanket, as though she was just another Indian woman returning to her family, worked better than expected. At first, Lucy was proud of herself for pulling off the ruse. No one had given her a second glance. Now she was thinking it might not have been a good idea.

As near as she could tell she'd only been walking for about twenty minutes. How far had she come, maybe a mile from the fort? Other than the wagon ruts, the last signs of civilization had just disappeared around the bend behind her. It was still a few miles to Quanah Parker's campsite on the edge of the Wichita Mountains.

What had she been thinking?

In the full light of day her plan to sneak off to Chief Parker's camp and hide with his wives now seemed foolish—at best. If Chief Parker would even allow it—which he almost certainly wouldn't—what did she hope to accomplish?

"Lucy, you goose." She admonished herself.

Running away to join the Indians was a childish notion and would endanger Quanah Parker and his family. Not to mention the fact she had no desire to live in a teepee in the middle of nowhere.

That thought brought her up short. Her romantic fancies about Yellow Horse hadn't included living in a teepee. Where did Yellow Horse live? Wasn't it somewhere in Texas?

As Lucy continued walking toward the mountains, she began to understand that her father had been right about her. She *was* behaving like a child, and all available evidence suggested she didn't know what she wanted.

The only thing she knew for sure was she didn't appreciate being treated like an unwelcome visitor in her father's life. She had to find a way to stay with him. Running away was not the way to convince him. It would only have the opposite effect. Whatever was she to do?

After the first hour or so, her valise had become quite heavy. She'd been changing it from one hand to the other. By now, both arms we feeling fatigued. Early on she'd discovered her shoes weren't meant for long hikes in the wilderness. More than once she'd put her foot wrong and nearly sprained an ankle.

She considered turning around and walking back. Instead, she decided to continue on the shorter distance to Chief Parker's camp where she could request a ride back to the fort. It would be both easier and safer. She almost laughed at the ridiculous picture she would make walking into the camp. How would she explain herself?

Shortly later, she heard the sound of approaching horses. Were Sergeant Major Jackson and his troopers out on patrol, looking for her? That would be fine with her. It would save further walking and they would have water. It might be a bit impractical though. How was she supposed to mount a horse in her dress and petticoats?

Lucy turned to greet the riders, only to discover they weren't anyone she knew.

Six men and a packhorse rode up to her. One of the men looked vaguely familiar, but she couldn't place him. They formed a circle around her.

"Well, well, well, this ain't something you see every day, now is it?" One of the men said.

"Whooeee, I reckon not. Damn, she's fine."

Looking around her, Lucy saw only rough men with horrible hygiene. She was appalled by their manners, or their lack of them. They should've at least taken off their hats.

"Good morning, gentlemen. I find myself alone and on foot. Could I trouble you to assist me?"

"Nope, but we may trouble you, on your back." The first man spoke again. He stepped off his horse and the others followed his lead. All except the man she'd seen somewhere before.

"I beg your pardon?" Lucy was frightened now.

"Hold on there, Zeb. I know this filly. She's the daughter of that army colonel over to Fort Sill."

"Don't mean squat to me." The first man said. He grabbed Lucy by her hair, pulling her to within inches of his face.

"She's a valuable prize, might be worth a fortune. You hurt her, or kill her, the army will dog us to hell, and hang us there."

Lucy remembered the speaker now. He was the leering passenger who bothered her on the stagecoach to Wichita Falls. His nose was more crooked than she remembered.

"What you sayin?" Zeb asked.

"We're too close to the fort. Let's grab her and git."

"Then what?"

"We'll take her to the boss. He'll know how to collect the ransom."

"He'll want her for himself. He can have what's left after we're done."

"Jim's right. We need to get out of here. We got no time to fool around," another man said. "If we can trade her for money, we can buy our own women. 'Sides, if this gal is important and we hurt her—the boss will skin us alive."

"I ain't afraid of him. Well, hell. Alright, girlie, you're coming with us."

Not knowing what else to do, Lucy screamed.

The man called "Zeb" hit her so hard; she felt an explosive blow to the side of her face, then nothing.

"Tie her up and throw her over the panniers on the pack horse, Scroggins. Tie her down good and tight, we don't want to lose our tasty little treat. Better throw a tarp over her. That pink dress can be seen for miles."

When Lucy regained consciousness she tried to scream again, but grubby hands stuffed a filthy bandana in her mouth and another was quickly tied in place to secure it. She tried to thrash, but found herself helpless, secured face down across the back of a horse, more or less wedged between the saw bucks of a pack saddle. The wood was pressing into the top of her hips. This condition made it difficult to breathe. Screaming was now impossible. In a moment even her vision was thwarted as a heavy canvas tarp was draped over and tucked in around her.

When the men were all mounted, Zeb Fletcher spat some orders.

"Scroggins, you ride back up this trail a quarter mile or so and then cut north. We'll meet you between here and the roost. If you touch that woman before I do, or if she gets loose, I'll kill you. You think on that."

DAN ARNOLD

CHAPTER 21

Riding out ahead of the herd, Yellow Horse neared the Red River. Seeing distant riders approaching, he stopped his horse. An army patrol was making a beeline toward him.

Experience had taught him to let the army come to him. Any act on his part would be interpreted as either aggressive or suspicious. Either situation would not be conducive to his continued good health. It wouldn't do to forget he was a Comanche off the reservation. He crossed his hands on the saddle horn and waited.

There were twelve men in the column, including a Tonkawa scout. There was no love lost between the Comanche and the Tonkawa.

When they were close enough, the buffalo soldiers spread out, forming a circle surrounding him.

For a moment they all sat and regarded each other.

He recognized some of the soldiers.

"Yellow Horse," Sergeant Major Jackson said, by way of greeting.

"Sergeant Major, is there something I can do for you?"

"We're searching for a missing civilian…Ahh, hell. It's Colonel Meadows' daughter, Lucy. She's gone missing from the fort. Have you seen her?"

Yellow Horse realized his jaw had dropped open.

"Out here? How would she get out here, and what do you mean, she's missing?"

Sergeant Major Jackson sighed.

"This morning, Colonel Meadows deployed with most of the regiment to pursue and apprehend Tu-ukumah and those with him. We had orders to escort Miss Meadows to Dodge City and see she boarded a train for the East. When I went to the Colonel's quarters to see if she was ready to go, or assist with her luggage, she wasn't there."

"That doesn't mean she's missing."

"We searched for her everywhere, and …she left a note. It's addressed to her father, the Colonel."

"Did you read it?"

Sergeant Major Jackson looked away, rubbing his mouth with one gauntleted hand.

"What does it say?"

The soldier sighed again, and then put his hand inside his tunic. He pulled out a folded piece of paper and handed it across to Yellow Horse.

Opening it, he read;

Dear Daddy,

I am not a child, nor am I an object you can carelessly discard. I am an adult woman and your daughter. I will be treated with respect. I am perfectly capable of choosing my own course in life. I choose to remain in the West, and so I will. Do not look for me. If in time you come to understand my feelings, I will learn of it and, if God so wills, we will be reunited.

Never doubt my love for you,

Lucy

"What's all this about, Sergeant Major?"

"The Colonel was sending her back east. I guess she didn't want to go."

"Wouldn't she be hiding somewhere at the fort? She spent most of her free time at the sutler's store."

"Nope. We searched every square inch and we questioned everyone. The ladies told us Miss Meadows was with them as the last of the troopers rode out. Less than an hour later, she was gone."

"People lie."

"Sure they do, but do you think they'd tell us such in the case of the Colonel's daughter? I can tell you her going missing has caused quite a stir."

Yellow Horse considered the possibilities. Lucy was headstrong and willful, but not a woman who would seek out partners in a scheme to defy her father. Whatever she'd done, she'd done it alone. It was that one fact that worried Yellow Horse more than any other. A woman alone had few resources.

"Have you been to see Quanah?"

"Yep. She ain't there either. You'll understand, I thought maybe she was looking for you. Chief Parker told us you would be bringing a herd this way today."

"I know she doesn't ride, but is there any way she could beg, borrow or steal a horse?"

"No, we looked into that too."

"She could've left the fort in a wagon or buggy."

"No."

"You rode all the way out here to tell me this. Do you really think she walked this far from the fort and waded across the river?"

"Well, no, of course not. Hell, Yellow Horse, it beats all I've ever seen. Nothing like this ever happened before."

"You'd better get word to the Colonel."

"I've sent a scout to overtake the column."

"Do you have any field glasses?"

"Yes."

"Give them to me. I'm going to talk to Quanah, and then I'll start scouting around."

"OK. If you're going that way, we'll swing south, then east searching the roads to outlying towns."

"You do that." Yellow Horse said, as he eased his horse between two troopers.

He was loping away as the soldiers regrouped.

DAN ARNOLD

CHAPTER 22

As Yellow Horse loped the Medicine Hat toward Quanah's campsite, his thoughts were centered on Lucy and where she might've gone. She knew very few people and almost all of them lived at Fort Sill.

The soldiers searched the fort, the surrounding area, even Quanah's camp, and she wasn't found.

She had to be somewhere.

Lucy wasn't clever enough to elude the Sergeant Major, but Quanah was smart enough to hide things from the entire United States Army. Could he, or would he, hide Lucy? No, Quanah was no fool. Keeping a white woman at his camp, especially the Colonel's daughter, would not be something he'd risk.

Did Lucy know that? Would she have tried to go to Quanah?

Sergeant Major Jackson told him there were no horses missing and no one had seen Lucy riding away. Other than those with the regiment, no wagons had left the fort. The women made it clear Lucy was with them when the last of the soldiers disappeared from view.

If she left the fort, she was probably on foot. If she were wrapped in a blanket, she might've been mistaken for an Indian woman. She knew the way, but it was a long walk to Quanah's camp.

Out here no man wanted to be set afoot, but Lucy wasn't a man and she had no idea what could happen to her. She could well be lost or injured somewhere?

There was only one way to find out.

Yellow Horse changed direction. He galloped toward the fort.

When he came to the wagon trail Quanah used to travel back and forth from the fort, he dismounted and began studying the ground.

Walking, he led the Medicine Hat for nearly a hundred yards before he found where a seep formed a little rivulet across the trail. Here on the edge of this damp ground he found the print of a white woman's shoe. It was Lucy's footprint. She'd been walking toward Quanah's camp, and only a short time, perhaps only four or five hours, previously.

Yellow Horse continued leading his horse, studying the ground with great care.

On occasion he found more sign.

Here, her foot had crumbled the edge of a wagon rut. There, she'd crushed a delicate herbaceous plant.

It frustrated Yellow Horse to have to move this slowly, but experience had taught him to be patient and let the signs lead him to his quarry. Although he knew Lucy was walking toward

Quanah's camp, he didn't want to miss something that might indicate she had left the wagon trail.

A little more than a mile from Quanah's camp, he came to a place where a pair of shod horses coming from the direction of the camp had intersected and covered Lucy's trail. The horse tracks veered away from the wagon ruts here and headed off cross country, turning back to the northwest, generally on a line back toward Quanah's camp.

Why would that be?

Whoever the riders were, they would almost certainly have encountered Lucy farther along the wagon trail.

Part of being a good tracker involved understanding what motivated the thing you were tracking, how it thought, and what it was most likely going to do.

This set of horse tracks was confusing. Something didn't seem right.

Who would meet a woman alone in the wilds and ride on by, then randomly change direction back across country in the general direction from which they'd just come?

Yellow Horse had to make a decision. Should he continue to follow the infrequent sign of Lucy's trail, or take off in pursuit of the two riders, hoping to overtake them and question them about Lucy?

He understood what motivated Lucy and it was clear she'd been headed for Quanah's camp.

He didn't understand the two sets of horse tracks. Who were the riders that left the wagon trail and what motivated them to do it?

CHAPTER 23

Yellow Horse slid the Medicine Hat to a stop in front of Quanah's teepee. Leaping off, he rushed past the women and children to scratch at the closed flap. Quanah opened the flap so quickly; he must've been in the process even as Yellow Horse approached.

"What's happened?" He asked in Comanche.

"Lucy Meadows has been taken."

"Taken where, by whom? The soldiers told me she was missing."

"I don't have much time to talk. Can I get some water, jerked meat and another horse?"

Quanah turned to one of the boys standing nearby. "Fetch my horse and one other. I will ride with Yellow Horse."

The women were already setting about gathering the things Yellow Horse requested.

"No, Quanah, you must stay. The herd will be here soon and the men must be paid. The army will be searching for her. I need you to tell them where I've gone."

"Where are you going?"

"The Wichitas. Listen, I gave my rifle away in Texas. Can I borrow one from you?"

A woman arrived with a parfleche and a canteen. She began using strips of rawhide to tie them on Yellow Horse's saddle.

Quanah motioned to Yellow Horse.

"Come inside."

Yellow Horse ducked into the teepee behind Quanah.

"Who took her?" Quanah asked as he sorted through some bundles.

"Probably white men, maybe Comancheros. All of the horses are shod with iron."

Quanah handed Yellow Horse a rifle in a buckskin sleeve and a box of cartridges.

Yellow Horse pulled the rifle part way out of the sleeve.

"This is the Winchester rifle General Sheridan presented to you at the surrender. It's the new model, '76."

"I like my old one better. I've never even fired that one you're holding. I figured it was mostly just for looking at."

Yellow Horse shook his head.

"When I bring it back, we'll talk rifles."

The two men hurried out of the teepee, as the boy brought up the horses. Quanah was carrying his saddle and a blanket.

"You will take my horse," he said, throwing the blanket on the animal. "Two Medicine Hats are better than one. Earlier this morning, one of my sons saw six men and a packhorse about a half mile east of here. They were going north."

"Must be them." Yellow Horse said, leaping back into his saddle. He took the reins of Quanah's horse from the boy.

Quanah finished saddling the animal and looked up at Yellow Horse.

"They were going slow. If you ride hard, you will come upon them before nightfall. Go with God."

"Thank you," Yellow Horse called over his shoulder as he galloped away.

He pushed his horse for a quarter mile, and then slowed to look for tracks. When he found the trail he slowed to a walk and stopped. After changing horses he set off on the new mount at a trot, both to let them get the feel for each other and so his horse could cool out. It also gave him an opportunity to study the tracks and get a sense of where they might be going.

Even just walking, six shod horses left a trail any child, at least any Comanche child, could follow across the prairie. It would become more challenging as they ascended into the rocky crags ahead. He'd been right; the outlaws were heading up into the Wichita Mountains.

After a few minutes he pushed Quanah's horse up into a lope, shortly later he was galloping toward the mountains, now coming into sharper focus.

As he rode, he thought about why the outlaws were traveling so slowly. It was a good sign. A sign that Lucy might still be alive. Somehow, she was slowing them down.

A horse walks at a speed of about three miles an hour. A trot can be about five miles an hour, and galloping like he was, even across this broken terrain, he was making about twenty miles an hour. The problem was, a horse carrying a rider couldn't maintain that pace for very long at a time. Being able to swap horses helped, but he had to balance his need for speed against the stamina and endurance of the horses.

Even so, he figured for every mile the outlaws traveled, he was gaining at least three.

The men who took Lucy had at least a three hour head start. That meant they were some ten miles or more beyond where he'd picked up their trail. By now, they'd be climbing into the Wichitas. At the speed he was going, he would cover that distance in thirty minutes.

***

"Zeb, someone's on our back trail." Lucy heard a man say.

The statement brought her mount to a stop. She was thankful for the break from the unending torture she'd endured since meeting these men.

Traveling cross country tied face down across the panniers on the pack horse was worse than anything she'd ever experienced.

Her hips were bruised by the sawbucks, and the ropes that bound her, chafed her flesh.

Under the tarp, the smell of the sweating animal was inescapable. At some point, she had wet herself. Her damp undergarments added to the stench. Breathing was difficult enough when the horse was only walking. When it trotted, she had to fight for every breath. The jarring of the trot made her feel as if her ribs were breaking and her insides were being shaken apart.

She'd become so thirsty, she was trying to suck her own saliva out of the bandana that nearly clogged her throat.

Since they'd begun the climb into the mountains, the shifting up and down angles had added a worsening level of misery.

"Where's he at?" Zeb Fletcher asked.

"Down there to the left, just beyond that outcrop, maybe a half a mile out behind us. He'll come out in the open…there he is."

"Huh, one man with two white horses. Gimmee that spyglass."

"Is he tracking us?"

"Yep, just as sure as shooting. Dressed like a white man, but I'll lay he's an Injun, probably an army scout."

"What should we do?"

Zeb Fletcher took off his hat and wiped his brow with his shirt sleeve.

"If he's on our trail, the army won't be far behind him. We'll split up from here and meet at the roost sometime tomorrow or the next day. Take your time and wander around some. I'll take the girl with me."

"Why?" Scroggins asked.

"He's too good a tracker. He stayed on our trail even up here in these rocks. We can't take a chance he'll follow one of us to the roost. You're the best shot with a rifle, Scroggins. You stay up here on this cliff and kill that Injun the minute he gets close enough to shoot."

With those last words, Lucy's mount began moving again.

***

Movement caught his eye. Yellow Horse scanned the rugged mountainside above him with the field glasses. There, about a half mile further up, men on horses, spreading out.

Yellow Horse cursed his carelessness. They'd spotted him before he saw them. There wasn't much he could do now. His prey would either scatter to the four winds or bushwhack him as he approached. He swung the horses into the rocks, taking a moment to consider what he should do. His next move would be dictated by what they were likely to do.

The smart move would be for them to ambush him while they had him outnumbered. The smarter move would be to leave the girl tied on the trail. He wouldn't be able to follow them, if he had to take Lucy to safety. Of course, the smartest move would've been never to take her at all.

Yellow Horse considered the men he was tracking to be lacking in smarts. Stupid men did stupid things. It made it difficult to anticipate what they might do next.

These men were not rational. Kidnapping the Colonel's daughter was foolhardy. Did they think they could hide from the United States Army? His people had lived on these lands for generations, yet even they'd been hunted down and forced to surrender.

He knew he was tracking the worst kind of renegade. These were men who had no sense of right or wrong. They would kill Lucy when they were done with her.

The only way he could hope to save Lucy was to think and act like they did. He figured they would wait in the rocks above him to kill him on sight.

They would show him no mercy. None would be given them.

DAN ARNOLD

CHAPTER 24

Jim Scroggins was a careful man. He prided himself on it. Trying to ambush the Indian in this rough country was not the sort of thing a careful man would do. On the other hand, crossing Zeb Fletcher was even more dangerous.

He'd wait a little while longer. If the Indian didn't show himself, he'd ride back to the dugout they called "the roost" empty handed. The boss would be angry, but it was a risk he'd have to take.

From up here on the rocky edge of the uplift he could see for miles. If the Indian was moving around below him somewhere he would be easy to spot. He should've come out in the open by now. The thing was-- the savage might not be below him. He could be up on this promontory with him.

He cussed to himself. He should've thought of it sooner. The sneaky red skin *was* here and somewhere close.

Scroggins cocked his rifle, listening. Except for a flight of crows far off in the distance, nothing moved.

The blow came as a complete surprise, knocking his rifle out of his hand, now broken at the wrist.

He reached to pull his pistol, but another blow from the rifle stock slammed the wind out of him and sent him toppling over the edge of the cliff. He bounced off a couple of boulders before landing in a heap some forty feet below, dazed and barely able to see.

***

Bending over the white man where he lay sprawled on the rocks at the base of the cliff, Yellow Horse observed two things. The man's body was broken, but he was still alive.

One eye was open, watching Yellow Horse. The other eye no longer functioned, destroyed by the shards of crushed bone surrounding it.

Through broken teeth the white man said, "You damned Injun. You've done for me."

"Not yet." Yellow Horse said. "First you will tell me where the woman is."

"No I won't. I aint tellin'you, nothin'."

Yellow Horse nodded and began gathering small twigs and leaves from the ground. He placed them in a pile and widened his search, returning with larger sticks, which he placed next to the pile of smaller material.

"What are you doing?" The man asked.

"It'll be dark soon. Nights get cold up here this time of year. I'll make a fire."

Yellow Horse walked away. He was gone longer this time. When he returned he carried limbs as thick as his wrists, broken off from dead cedar and mesquite trees.

He knelt and began building the fire. As he worked, he looked over at the injured man.

"Where is the woman?"

The man slowly shook his head.

"By now, the shock has worn off. The pain is setting in. You are hurt bad, but not hurt to death. Although many bones are broken, you are not paralyzed. The smallest movement will be horribly painful. You can't stand, probably can't even crawl. In time you would starve or freeze to death here in these rocks, but not tonight. Tonight we will talk. Tell me where the woman is."

"You go to hell."

"Where is the Colonel's daughter?"

The white man tried to chuckle, but it rattled out as a cough.

"Like I said, go to hell."

Yellow Horse sighed and resumed building the fire.

"This hell you mentioned? The nuns spoke of this. A place of unending suffering, I think. Me? …Maybe, someday. Today, it is *you* who have arrived at the gates of hell."

Arranging the loose leaves and twigs as tinder, he built a small teepee frame over it with other twigs. He popped a match and lit it.

As the flames began to consume the twigs he added larger ones, then sticks. Now the fire was burning well, without any visible smoke.

He remained squatted down, facing the injured man on the other side of the fire.

"It's getting dark. Tell me where the woman is."

"No."

Yellow Horse stood and walked over to the white man.

"Unless you tell me, I will hurt you."

"Go on, do it. I'll never tell."

"You will. I'm going to make you."

The man closed his one remaining eye.

Yellow Horse bent and grabbed one of the man's feet, yanking his leg straight.

The man screamed and nearly fainted, breaking out in a sweat.

"Where is the woman?"

The man was panting for breath

"Why, why do you care?"

Yellow Horse tugged on the man's boot, ignoring the expressions of pain, until he pulled it all the way off. There was no sock. The exposed foot was impossibly white, like the belly of a fish.

Returning to the fire, he squatted and set the boot down beside him. He waited until the man was breathing normally again.

"Lucy Meadows is gentle and soft. She can't survive here without help."

The white man didn't understand.

"So? What's it to you?"

Yellow Horse pulled a stick about as thick as his thumb out of the fire. He stood and blew on the smoldering end until it glowed, cherry red.

"I know her. She is a good woman. What you would call a Christian. Tell me where she is."

The man just shook his head.

Walking back over to the injured man, Yellow Horse grabbed the exposed foot.

He blew on the stick again.

"No, don't do it. Please don't. It ain't Christian."

"No, it ain't."

"Wait, wait. Aieeegh!"

Yellow Horse wrinkled his nose at the smell of burning flesh. Dropping the foot, he turned back to the fire and squatted again.

He watched the panting and whimpering white man. When he'd settled down enough to listen, Yellow Horse pulled another stick from the fire and blew on it.

As he approached the quivering man, now staring at him with his one remaining eye, wide open, Yellow Horse said, "We can do this all night. Now, tell me. Where did they take her?

DAN ARNOLD

CHAPTER 25

The sun was low in the western sky when Zeb Fletcher arrived at the roost with the packhorse.

"You have any luck?" Jason Vazquez asked him as the man drew up in front of the dugout.

"Yep, we cleaned em out, just like we done to that settlement over in Texas. Them Injuns didn't have much, but we took everything they had, didn't leave no witnesses neither."

Fletcher stepped off his horse, tying it to a fence post.

"Wait'll you see what I brung you, Boss."

"Where are the others?"

"I told em to spread out and come in one at a time."

"That might be the smartest thing you ever did."

"I didn't want to take a chance on being tracked. There was some Injun following us."

Fletcher began untying the cords holding the tarp down on the pack horse.

"I thought you said you killed em all."

"We did, this Injun crossed our path as we were coming into the mountains. Let me show you what I brung you, Boss."

He threw the tarp back.

Vazquez took a step forward.

"A woman? Is she dead? She stinks to high heaven."

Zeb Fletcher grabbed Lucy's hair and lifted her head up.

"Naw, she ain't dead. She's a looker too, don't you think?"

Lucy tried not to show her fear or her humiliation, but the hot tears gave her away. When Fletcher let go of her hair, she hung her head and prayed.

Jason Vazquez nodded and spat on the ground.

"She is that, but having a woman here will cause trouble. Why'd you bring her?"

"She ain't just any woman, Boss. This here is Colonel Meadows' daughter. Scroggins said she's worth a ton of money. He said you'd know how to get it."

"Where's Scroggins?"

"I left him to kill the Injun who was following us. I reckon he might've been an army scout."

"Army scout, did you lead the army up here?"

"Naw, he was just a lone Injun with two white, pinto horses."

"White horses, are you sure?"

"Yep, I got a real good look at em with the spyglass."

"That was no army scout. They don't ride white horses. Army scouts like to be sneaky. You know, blend in. Among the Indians, only great warriors have flashy horses like that. The only war chief around here, with a horse like you describe, is Quanah Parker."

"Well, whoever he was, he's a good Injun, now."

"Why would Quanah Parker be following you? He's Comanche. What kind of Indians did you rob?"

"Kickapoos or Kiowas, I think. It was way over east of here. Besides, it don't matter. Like I say, he's a dead Injun, now."

"He'd better be. Bring that gal inside."

Zeb Fletcher loosened the ropes and dragged Lucy off the pack saddle, dropping her like a sack of flour.

She tried to stand, hoping to make a run for it, but her battered and bruised body failed her. She only managed to get up on her hands and knees.

Fletcher grabbed her hair at the nape of the neck, hauling her to her feet. When she staggered and fell, he dragged her by her hair the rest of the way through the gap in the rocks that served as the doorway into the dugout.

Once inside, Fletcher flung Lucy to the floor of the dugout, as though she were a bag of refuse.

Sitting up she found herself in a single room about ten feet wide and sixteen feet long. The walls were made of stacked rock and earth, rising about six feet to the roofline. The roof was built of poles laid across a central beam that was just a single downed tree, from which the limbs and branches had been crudely chopped away.

Cowhides lay across the poles, with rocks and earth piled on top. The cowhides had once been stiffened, dried rawhide, but were now sagging and green with mold.

The dugout stank of filth, unwashed bodies, wood smoke, rotting cowhide, and other unidentified disgusting odors.

A single kerosene lantern, sitting atop a table fashioned from boards laid across a couple of barrels, provided the only illumination.

At the back of the room, there was a sort of natural cave where huge boulders had piled up in an ancient rock slide, leaving an open space between them. From the filthy blankets lying on the dirt floor back there, she judged that space to be the sleeping quarters.

Looking down at Lucy where she knelt on the rocky floor, the hideously ugly man the outlaw had called "Boss", sneered.

"Welcome to our mansion on the hill, girlie. What, you don't like our cozy little roost? I expect you're used to something a bit nicer. Still, it got us through the winter. Had to bring the horses in here on the coldest nights, but we made it through."

Lucy saw bridles, hides, odds and ends of clothing, and even dead game hanging from the rafters. A low fire burned over in a corner. The smoke rose through a pipe jammed up through the roof. The floor space against the walls was mostly occupied by crates and barrels doing double duty as storage and furniture.

Three saddles were stacked on an empty barrel turned on its side. Saddle blankets were stuffed into the smashed open end.

"What's your name, gal?" The ugly man asked as Zeb Fletcher removed the filthy rags that gagged her.

Lucy couldn't answer if she wanted to. Her mouth and throat were too parched.

"Not talking, huh? I'll bet you can scream though. Shall I make you scream?"

Lucy's startled expression and fierce shaking of her head seemed to amuse him.

"Don't worry yourself, honey. I expect you'll scream some, before we're finished with you."

"Let me have her, Boss. In about one minute, I'll get some sound out of her."

"All in good time, Fletcher, we'll wait till we know who she is, and what she's worth."

"I told you, she's the Colonel's daughter."

"Is that true, sweetie?"

Lucy nodded and tried to speak.

"I, I'm Lucy Meadows," she croaked.

"Well then, Lucy, what do you think your daddy would pay to get you back?"

"I, I don't know."

"I figure he'd pay fifty thousand dollars for a fine gal like you. Do you reckon he's good for it?"

Lucy had no way of knowing whether her father could pay so much money. She wondered if he would even want to get her back. With more hot tears streaming down her face, she shook her head.

"He better find some way to come up with the money, or he'll never see you again."

"Hell, he ain't never gonna see her again, either way." Fletcher said. "I say we have our fun, and cut her throat."

"No. We're not going to do that. Colonel Meadows won't come across with the money if he thinks we've already killed her. He'll want some proof she's still alive. How old are you, honey?"

"I'm twenty years old."

"Married?"

"No sir."

"Strange, a fine looking gal like you not married yet. You must either be a floozy or mean as a snake. Well, either way, just because we can't kill you, it don't mean we can't have our fun. Fletcher's been on some raids, here lately. He's had him an Injun gal or two. Me, I ain't even seen a woman all winter. Winter is sure enough over now.

Crawl over here to me. I'm fixin' to show you something you'll never forget."

Lucy closed her hand over a sharp stone. She had no intention of allowing these bearded pigs to so much as touch her without a fight. She'd die first.

DAN ARNOLD

CHAPTER 26

The sun was now high enough in the sky to call it morning.

Yellow Horse admired the clever way the dugout was concealed at the edge of an ancient rock slide in a hanging canyon. Without knowing where to look, no routine cavalry patrol or U.S. Marshal would ever find this narrow, hidden canyon.

A cedar thicket obscured the approach from the bottom. The outlaws never came in that way. They made their way up, through the rocks and brush on the other side of the mountain. A lone man standing at the top of the ridgeline could see all the lower ground for miles, beyond the cedars.

If the broken and dying white man hadn't told him how to find the hideout, Yellow Horse would still be carefully searching for the tracks of the man leading the pack horse. He'd still be on the trail.

As it was, he hated that Lucy had gone without rescue overnight. He didn't even know if she was still alive.

There were four horses in the makeshift corral. If one was the packhorse, it suggested there were at least three men here.

It was time to reduce that number by one.

Too late, the lookout turned. His eyes flared as the steel blade drove up into his brain, the bowie knife buried to the hilt behind his bearded chin. Jerking his knife free, Yellow Horse let the man's body fall where it was.

Here on the ridge, Yellow Horse waited for a moment, watching the dugout below.

He was about to start working his way down, when a rider appeared between two boulders on the other side of the ravine.

The man stopped, waiving his hat.

Not knowing what else to do, Yellow Horse raised his rifle in the air in response.

The rider was expecting some sort of acknowledgement from the lookout. It was enough. He wasn't paying much attention to who the "lookout" was. He began weaving his way through the rocks and brush, down toward the dugout.

There was no time to wait. Other outlaws would be coming.

Silently moving as fast as the conditions allowed, Yellow Horse raced down the side of the ravine.

He arrived in the brush at the edge of the corral, just as the rider dismounted. Before he could attack, the cowhide covering was thrown away from the doorway of the dugout.

Yellow Horse dropped where he was, concealed by the brush.

"Rogers, about time you showed up. Keep an eye on this gal. She needs to squat in the bushes."

A big, rough looking man with a beard, and a bad cut down the side of his face, pulled Lucy through the doorway, shoving her to the ground.

"Howdy, Boss. Sure, I'll see she don't get away."

"If she does…"

"She won't."

The evident leader of the outlaws dropped the cowhide back in place as he disappeared into the dugout.

Lucy lay cowering in the dust as the outlaw tied his horse by the bridle reins. Her face was covered by her long, blonde hair, now down and in disarray. She hung her head as he walked up to her.

The man reached down, dragging her to her feet by one arm. He shoved her toward some rocks and brush on the other side of the dugout.

Yellow Horse got a quick glimpse of her battered face and torn clothing.

"Get in there and do what you gotta do. If you ain't back here in about one minute, I'll come get you."

The man stood watching Lucy as she moved off into the rocks and brush.

Knowing he would never get a better chance, Yellow Horse crouched and dashed forward past the front of the dugout. Clamping his hand over the man's mouth, he sliced the bowie knife across the outlaw's throat, cutting deep, from one side to the other.

The man was quick. He had his pistol out in about one second, but as his blood sprayed out in front of him, he dropped it, grabbing his neck with both hands. With a gurgling sound, he dropped to his knees. A moment later he fell to one side.

Yellow Horse looked at his own blood soaked hands. He used two fingers on each hand to paint bloody stripes across his cheeks.

Looking up, he found Lucy staring at him. Her pale face, and wide eyes, expressed her shock and horror.

He put a bloody finger to his lips, and then, holding both crimson stained hands up, indicated she should stay where she was.

Her only response was to blink and sway.

Leaving her, Yellow Horse slipped past the front of the dugout, back to the corral. He cut the reins on the tied horse, and then eased the single pole away from the opening of the corral.

After retrieving his rifle, he returned to Lucy where she remained transfixed, staring at the dead outlaw. He grabbed her hand, and began leading her up the side of the arroyo.

Nearing the top, they heard a shout. Looking back, Yellow Horse saw the loose animals scatter as a man attempted to catch the saddled one. The leader emerged from the dugout, looking around.

With no further need for stealth, Yellow Horse urged Lucy over the ridgeline.

Two questions owned his thoughts; would they reach the horses before they were overtaken, and if they did, could Lucy stay on a galloping horse?

DAN ARNOLD

CHAPTER 27

The horses were hidden about a quarter of a mile from the outlaw's roost. By the time she and Yellow Horse reached them, Lucy was about done in.

Her haunted expression, torn clothing, and beaten and bruised face told Yellow Horse what her plight had been over the long hours of the night.

He took the canteen and the parfleche from his horse. Handing the canteen to Lucy, he said, "We'll rest here for a moment. Are you hungry?"

Lucy was drinking as though she hadn't seen water in a week.

Yellow Horse took the canteen from her.

"Easy does it. Let's see what we have to eat."

The parfleche contained some jerked meat and pemmican.

"What's that?" Lucy asked, pointing at the somewhat sticky substance.

"Fresh pemmican, this is made with dried venison, tallow and crushed berries. The berries are just now ripe, so it was made in the last few days. It'll last for weeks."

"What's it for?"

"It's food, Lucy. A little pemmican can keep you going for days."

"I haven't eaten in two days."

"For now, we'll settle for jerky. If we don't find a cavalry troop first, later on I'll cook us up some pemmican stew. Here break off some of this jerky and chew on it. When it's gone, I'll give you some more. We've got to move. Do you think you could sit on my horse?"

Lucy was gnawing on a piece of jerky, but she nodded her head.

"Ok. Grab the saddle horn. When I lift you, swing your leg over. I'll fix the stirrups for you once you're in the saddle."

"Wait, James. You killed that man. Why? I mean, how? How could you take his life?"

"If I had more time, I'd have taken his scalp. We'll talk about it later. Up you go."

Once Lucy was situated, Yellow Horse mounted Quanah's horse. Taking the reins of Lucy's mount he set off at a walk. Lucy clung to the saddle horn with both hands, swaying dangerously at every turn.

Yellow Horse wanted to gallop out of the mountains, but Lucy wasn't ready. Even so, they'd have to move more swiftly than a walk.

"Lucy, we're going to go faster now. Lean forward a little and grab my horse's mane with one hand. Hold on tight, here we go."

Knowing Lucy would bounce off at a trot, Yellow Horse urged Quanah's horse up into a lope. Looking back, he was glad to see his own horse immediately follow suit.

Lucy was doing as instructed, almost lying on the horse's neck, holding on for dear life. If they had to stop suddenly she would fly right out of the saddle, over the Medicine Hat's head. Going down a steep grade, she would probably fall off. The rocks and brush would show no mercy.

"Lucy, Try to sit up. That saddle horn will hurt you. Put some weight in those stirrups. That's the way. You're doing fine."

He was trying to coach Lucy, maintain the fastest pace possible, and choose the way forward through the broken and inhospitable landscape, all while expecting a rifle shot at any moment.

Several times he had to slow for steep terrain and changes of direction. On more than one occasion Lucy nearly fell off. After an hour or so, Yellow Horse drew up.

Scanning the area for potential threats, he said, "We'll sit here for a little while and let the horses rest. Are you OK?"

Lucy didn't answer. She'd withdrawn into herself. Yellow Horse had seen this before. It was the result of the hardship and trauma she'd endured. Her reserves were depleted, her strength exhausted.

With a sigh, he considered what must be done. He figured they'd only traveled about six miles, even less, as the crow flies. They were nearing the promontory where he'd encountered the outlaw left behind to ambush him. If the others were tracking him and Lucy, within a few minutes, they'd find them here. This was not a good place to make a fight, and he wouldn't be able to see them coming.

"Lucy, I know you're tired. We have to keep going. We're going to climb for a little while, just a few minutes, and then we'll rest. Hang on. Here we go."

When they reached the promontory, Yellow Horse stopped and dismounted. Lucy collapsed into his arms as he pulled her from the saddle. She was limp and unresponsive. He laid her on the ground while he spread out his bedroll, and then he scooped her up and made her as comfortable as he could. He looked at her for a long moment, where she lay wrapped in his blanket, before he set about scanning their back trail for any sign of the outlaws.

He couldn't see anything moving. He circled the top of the mountain hoping to spot a cavalry patrol, but no riders were anywhere to be seen.

Returning to Lucy, he found her sleeping. He unsaddled the horses and built a fire. They weren't going to be able to travel anymore. Lucy was too weak to go on.

As he sat watching her he realized what he would have to do. Lucy needed more help than he could give her. While this was a good place to look out, or make a fight, it was too exposed to the elements for Lucy's health and welfare. He needed to get her back to her people.

Rising, he drew his bowie knife. Soon, two cedar trees of about twelve feet each fell to his chopping. He used the knife to strip the limbs off.

As a child he'd learned how to make small, nearly smokeless fires, never using more wood than was needed. The white man liked to make big, blazing fires, and seemed to care little how much smoke was produced.

After another tour of the mountain top, Yellow Horse returned to the fire and began adding green cedar boughs. The flames leapt up, and white smoke rose in a growing column. He continued adding greenery, brush and debris, creating a darker smudge that would be visible for miles in every direction.

He was hoping the smoke would alert an army patrol. He used a saddle blanket to interrupt the column in an unmistakable series, creating a signal any army scout would be able to read.

If the signal attracted the outlaws, fine, he would see them coming. The resulting gunfire would help draw in the cavalry.

An hour or so later, his efforts were rewarded.

***

Lucy thrashed and moaned in her sleep as Yellow Horse watched the riders approaching from below.

The first rider to reach them was a Tonkawa scout. He sat his horse as he assessed the situation. He glanced at Yellow Horse, and nodded an almost imperceptible show of grudging respect.

Colonel Meadows, Lieutenant Fitzpatrick, and a dozen troopers soon clambered up to join them.

The Colonel rushed to Lucy's side, as Lieutenant Fitzpatrick directed the troopers to take up defensive positions.

Lucy awakened to her father's impassioned pleas, but she was confused, frightened and disoriented.

Lieutenant Fitzpatrick drew Yellow Horse aside.

"Thank God you found her. Did they…I mean, was she…?"

"She didn't say, and I didn't ask. If it's important to you, ask her yourself."

Colonel Meadows stood and addressed the lesser officer.

"Lieutenant Fitzpatrick, choose six troopers and go in pursuit of the men who did this."

"Yes sir. Where are they, Yellow Horse?"

"I don't know."

"What do you mean, you don't know? How did you find Lucy, I mean Miss Meadows?"

"I know where they were, but they know the army is searching for her. I expect by now they've taken flight in three or four different directions. You don't have enough men to follow all those different trails.

Colonel, you need to get Lucy to Fort Sill. She's too weak to ride. I cut those two cedar poles. Have a couple of your men run them through the sleeves of their tunics. It'll make a suitable litter or travois. You can use my horse to pull the travois."

The colonel nodded.

"Yes, of course. You're right. I'm sorry, Yellow Horse. I haven't even thanked you for rescuing my daughter. I don't know where to start."

"Start by getting her back to the fort, safe and sound."

"Will you come back with us?"

"No. I have other plans. I'll stop in and see Lucy in a few days. Will you arrange it so my horse is taken care of until I return?"

"Certainly I will, as if it were my own."

With a nod, Yellow Horse began saddling Quanah Parker's horse. Another Tonkawa scout arrived and conferred with the first man. The two of them walked over to speak to Yellow Horse.

"This man tells me he found the body of a white man down in the rocks below. Do you know what happened to him?"

"Yes."

"How did he die?"

Yellow Horse tightened the cinch as he glanced at the scout.

"He fell from up here."

"Yes, but this man says the white man had been burned."

Yellow Horse led the horse a few steps away from the two men and mounted.

"He wouldn't tell me where to look for Lucy, but then he did, right at the end."

The two Tonkawas looked at each other, and then shrugged. Evidently they felt ono need to speak of this to the Colonel.

Yellow Horse nodded his thanks, and rode away.

CHAPTER 28

Quanah Parker looked up in response to a call from one of his wives. Ten days had passed since Yellow Horse borrowed his rifle and his horse to search for Lucy Meadows. More than a week since Lucy was returned to Fort Sill. In all that time, there was no sign of Yellow Horse.

Now, here he was.

With a frown, Quanah watched the rider approach. He frowned because the man looked so different from when he'd last seen him. His long brown hair was loose about his shoulders. He had no hat, and the lower half of his face was blackened with war paint. Most disturbing of all was the war lance he carried, from which hung four, fresh, scalps.

"Hello, Yellow Horse. It's past time you showed up. How are you?"

"I am well, Quanah."

"Are you? You look terrible. What have you done?" He pointed at the scalps.

"Only what needed to be done."

"No. Those days are done. If the army saw you, they would arrest you on the spot. Do you want to be imprisoned, or hung?"

"No, but I could not let evil go unpunished."

"Evil? This thing you have done, is it not evil?"

"It is just."

"No, Yellow Horse, it is not justice that sent you on the war path. It is vengeance. Evil for evil is not the way."

"It is my way."

Quanah sighed, shaking his head. He reached out, grasping the cheek piece of the bridle.

"Thank you for returning my horse and rifle. Step down. We'll get you cleaned up and fed, and then we'll talk."

"Yes, we will talk."

***

Once Yellow Horse was fed, and all sign of the war paint removed, he sat with Quanah in his lodge.

"…It was the only gift I could give him. So, now you owe me a rifle."

Quanah considered the story of how he'd come to have four shorthorn bulls in his herd. After a moment, he nodded.

"Yes, you did the right thing. You should keep the fancy rifle General Sheridan gave me. I will do something for you. Leave your war lance with me. It is crudely made anyway. The scalps too, you must not be caught with those. I owe you that, at least."

"Is someone looking for me?"

"Waiting-- would be a better word."

"I must go to the fort to retrieve my horse."

"Yes, your horse. Why have you not asked about the Colonel's daughter?"

"How is she?"

"She is recovered, thanks to you."

Yellow Horse looked away.

"From some things, a person cannot recover."

"She has her strength back. Healing from the ordeal will happen in time. From now on, where ever she goes and whatever she does, she owes her life to you. Do not be deceived. Where there is life, there is always hope. You gave her that."

"It was the will of the Great Spirit."

"That part was. How many men have you killed in the days you've been away?"

"You see the scalps. These men did much worse. They were the same men who wiped out the settlement in Texas."

"Was that not a matter for the white man's law?"

"They killed others, from among our people. Do you believe the white man's law would do anything about that?"

"Yes, I do. Here in the Territory, the army, or the United States Marshals, would've arrested them for their crimes. If they were in Texas, wouldn't your friend John Sage or the Rangers go after them?"

"Yes, but no court of law would convict them for killing Indians."

Quanah sighed. There was some truth to that statement.

"Perhaps not, but they would hang them for what they did to Lucy Meadows."

"I saved them the trouble."

"Yellow Horse, you must not go on like this."

"I am done with the war path. This matter is concluded."

"Is it?"

"Yes. I see your cattle on the range. Did you pay the cowboys?"

"I did, fifteen dollars a head, plus another two dollars a head for providing the cowboys, remuda and cook wagon."

Yellow Horse shook his head and chuckled.

"What is so funny?"

"Charlie Goodnight."

"I don't understand."

"It's not important. Did the cowboys all go back to Texas?"

"All but one, the man called John Reynolds Hughes. He stayed to wait for you."

"Why? We had no such arrangement."

"He is interested in our people and our heritage. He asks many questions. He seems like a good man."

"Yes, he is. He's spent time among our people before. Where is he now?"

"He rode to Fort Sill, yesterday."

"I must go there."

"You can go tomorrow. Tonight we will smoke the pipe, speak words of truth, and pray."

"That sounds like the old ways, Quanah. I thought you are a Christian."

"I am Christian. You are not. If you were a Christian, you would not seek out your enemies to kill them. Christians understand how to forgive an enemy, even love them."

Yellow Horse stared into the fire for a time. When he spoke, he was very solemn.

"Making war on our enemies is the Comanche way. It is the way of the warrior, blood for blood, evil for evil.

You have been a great warrior, Quanah. If you can speak of loving an enemy, you really have changed."

"Is it so hard for you to understand?"

"Yes."

"It starts with realizing that all people under the sun are flawed, including you and me. The Christians call this 'sin'. We both know, in every tribe, there are good people and bad. Even good people sometimes do bad things. As Comanche, we think only of making war. We think we are good and our enemies are bad. If I can learn to look at our enemy and see myself in them, it becomes more difficult to hate. If I don't hate, perhaps I can love."

"This is strong medicine."

"Yes."

"What about justice? If you forgive your enemy, there is no justice."

"I think there are two kinds of justice. Creator's justice is not the same as the justice of human beings."

"I am only a man. I do justice according to the customs of our people."

"Maybe it is time for our customs to change."

Yellow Horse was stunned.

"This is a hard saying. I must think about it."

Quanah grinned at Yellow Horse.

"You and me both, I think about it every day."

CHAPTER 29

With the sunrise, Quanah and his whole family traveled to Fort Sill. Yellow Horse drove one of the wagons.

As was his custom, Quanah parked the wagons at the edge of the parade ground.

Yellow Horse trotted up the stairs of the headquarters building. He paused to explain to the sentries who he was and what business he had with Colonel Meadows.

When he was escorted into the Colonel's office, he found the man standing behind his desk, waiting to shake his hand.

"Yellow Horse, it's good to see you. We were starting to worry. Would you like a cigar?"

"No thank you, Colonel. What were you worrying about?"

"You said you'd be coming to see Lucy in a few days. It's been more than a week."

"My business took longer than expected. How is she?"

"She's alive, thanks to you. The ordeal has changed her. She's more thoughtful now. I suppose she's more…reserved, even withdrawn. She doesn't visit with the other ladies on the post. Alice Jones, the Agent's wife, comes to visit her, nearly every day. Other than that, she reads her Bible.

About the only place she goes is to the livery stable to check on your horse. Lucy does that, first thing, every morning. I believe she's made some kind of connection with that animal. Let's go see her."

"May I stop by, later? I have to get some things at the store. Then, I'll be along."

"That's fine. How long will you be here at the fort?"

"I'll only be here today. I have to go back to Texas and rejoin the Rangers. I'm overdue."

"I'm sorry to hear that. Lucy will be disappointed."

"Will she? I figured she'd rather not see me."

"Why do you say that?"

After all that's happened…Colonel, she saw me kill a man."

"I know, she told me. I say good riddance to bad rubbish. You only did what you had to do, to save my daughter. I'm forever in your debt."

"Does she think less of me?"

"No, I don't believe she does. Pardon my saying so, Yellow Horse. Aren't these are things you should discuss with her?"

"Yes sir, I will."

"Good man. May I walk with you to the store? It's on the way to my quarters."

"Yes, of course."

As they were walking, Colonel Meadows said, "All of this is partially my fault, you know?"

"How is that, Colonel?"

"After you told Captain Lee where to look for Tu-ukumah and his men, we sent scouts to find them. Once they were located, we set out to capture them. I'd arranged for Lucy to go back East, but I hadn't included her in my planning, or even discussed it with her. I should've known better. She's just like her mother."

"It was very foolish of her to set out alone and on foot."

"Yes, very. She knows it now. When we learned Lucy was missing, I left Captain Lee in command of the 10th with orders to proceed as planned. Lieutenant Fitzpatrick asked permission to return with me to search for Lucy. Given their relationship, I granted it. He and I returned to the fort with the courier."

"How did you find us in the mountains?"

"Quanah sent one of his sons to tell us you were headed into the Wichita Mountains, on the trail of the men who took her.

By then it was late in the day. We bivouacked for the night about six miles from where we saw your smoke signal the next morning."

They stopped at the bottom of the stairs leading up to the store.

"Has Tu-ukumah been captured?"

"Yes, Captain Lee captured him and most of his band, three days ago. We got word this morning. You'll have to tell me how you were able to find Lucy and rescue her from those outlaw renegades."

They started up the stairs.

"I'm a pretty good tracker."

"So I've heard.

At the door, Colonel Meadows opened it, motioning for him to go in first. Inside, every eye in the store turned to Yellow Horse. All conversation stopped. Evidently word of his part in the rescue of Colonel Meadows' daughter had spread.

Moving past the customers, Colonel Meadows walked directly to the counter and spoke to the sutler.

"Store keep, give this man anything he asks for, and charge it to me."

"No, Colonel, that's not…"

The Colonel raised his hand, cutting Yellow Horse off.

"Please, it's the least I can do. When you get done here, we'll see you at my quarters."

CHAPTER 30

When Yellow Horse stepped out of the store, the first thing he saw was Lucy Meadows. She was playing tag with Quanah's children on the parade ground. Quanah and the Comanche women looked on. Lucy wore a dark blue dress with some sort of silver pattern woven into it. Her blonde hair was pinned up under a silly blue hat, cocked over to one side of her head. She was so involved in the game she didn't see him approaching.

"Tag, you're it," he said, tapping her on the shoulder.

To his surprise she rushed into his arms, embracing him with more intensity than he would've believed she was capable.

Shuddering sobs wracked her body, prompting him to wrap his arms around her.

Quanah and the women began gathering up the children, who were gazing at them with mixtures of curiosity and mirth.

After a moment Lucy stepped back.

"I…I'm sorry, James. I must look a mess. I've just been so worried you would never come back. Are you OK?"

"Yes, I'm fine."

"I see you have another new hat."

"You do, too."

She smiled and gazed into his eyes for a moment.

"I've been keeping an eye on your horse. You know, I never learned his name. What is it?"

"It's a Comanche word that means sunlight, shining on a smooth rock."

"Oh. You'll have to teach it to me. I thought it might be something like 'Wind Dancer'.

"Hmmm, it's not a very mighty name for a warrior's horse. Still, I think I like that name better. Wind Dancer it is."

"Let's go see him, shall we?"

"Yes, I'd like that."

As they walked along, Lucy reached out, taking his rough hand in her gloved one. It was a strange and surprisingly intimate feeling to Yellow Horse.

As they reached the livery stable, Lucy said, "Now that you're back, we can start planning our picnic."

"What picnic is that?"

"You promised to take me out to see one of the big cattle herds going up the trail."

They stopped at the paddock where "Wind Dancer" was munching hay in the company of a couple other horses. Yellow Horse called out in Comanche, causing the Medicine Hat to lift his head. Seeing Yellow Horse and Lucy, the big pinto came trotting over to the fence.

As Lucy petted the animal, Yellow Horse considered how to approach the subject he wanted to talk about.

"Do you think I'm a horrible person?"

"No. whatever makes you think that?"

"I've done things…"

"Shhhhh, I don't want to talk about it."

"We must talk about it. What those men did…I killed them all, Lucy."

"Oh. No! Oh, Yellow Horse, please tell me you didn't."

"I did. Quanah says it is not the way of a Christian. You are a Christian. Can you understand why I did it?"

Tears began to trickle from her eyes as she looked at him.

"Yes, I understand. Do you understand it was wrong to do?"

"Quanah says Christians know how to forgive. After what you've suffered, could you forgive those men?"

Lucy looked away. After a moment she said, "I can't forget, not yet, but forgive? Yes, I have to. I can't let hatred or bitterness poison my soul. It's tempting, to hate them.

It was all so…horrific. When they kidnapped me, I prayed God would spare me. I prayed he would somehow free me. When I was out there, in that place…I wanted to kill them myself. In the moment, I tried to. I slashed their leader with the only weapon I could find. He knocked me out. Later, I prayed God would let me die.

Yellow Horse hung his head.

Lucy reached out and lifted his chin, looking into his eyes.

"Thanks to you, I'm still alive. I believe God sent you to rescue me. I've had time to reflect on it since then. I've learned things about myself. I'm strong in ways I never imagined, and I'm weak in ways I was blind to, before…

"I'm sorry I couldn't get there sooner…"

"No. Never be sorry. I owe you my life. The Bible says, 'We know that all things work together for good to them that love God, to them who are the called according to his purpose.'

I believe good will come from this. If I allow hatred and bitterness to consume me, I'll miss the good. So, I have to find it in my heart to forgive them. I forgive you."

Yellow Horse was staggered. He was nearly overcome with emotion. It was not the way of a warrior to cry in the presence of a woman.

He looked away and changed the subject.

"I have to go to Texas. I promised to return to my Ranger Company. They expected me to come back, long ago."

Lucy's eyes flared and her mouth opened. She wiped away the tears from her face, a face that now showed little emotion.

"I see. When will you go?"

"Today, right away, in fact."

"It seems like you're always riding off somewhere. Will you come back soon?"

"I don't know. It depends on what work I must do."

Lucy put both hands on his face, kissing him full on the mouth.

Yellow Horse responded, wrapping her in his arms.

When she pulled away, Lucy smiled.

"Well, I hope that will help you decide to come back, immediately. I'll be waiting."

"Lucy, I can't promise to come back soon. I might not be able to come back at all."

Lucy frowned.

"Just to be clear, James Yellow Horse, you are not my only suiter. I will wait for you, but there's a limit to how long. If you aren't back in one week, I'll assume you don't care for me."

"I'll try, but my life is…complicated."

Lucy glared at him, crossing her arms.

"One week. If you aren't back in one week, don't bother coming back, ever."

CHAPTER 31

John Everett Sage and the four Rangers with him stopped to watch the lone rider approaching from the hilltop ahead of them.

As the horseman drew up in front of them, Sage removed his hat, wiping sweat and dust from his brow.

"Good afternoon, Yellow Horse. What brings you out here? We haven't seen you in, oh I don't know, a month?"

"Yes, more or less. I'm sorry, John, I got held up. It took me three days to find you."

"Yeah, we've been busy." Jim Gillett said.

"It appears today you're headed for Palo Duro Canyon."

"Yep, good guess. Charlie Goodnight sent for us. Somebody stole a bunch of his horses yesterday evening."

"I have a bone to pick with him."

"Business or personal?"

"Both."

Sage nodded and said, "So, what held you up? You haven't found a girlfriend have you?"

Yellow Horse opened his mouth to answer, but closed it again.

"Hah! I told you it was a woman. I win the bet, Cap'n." Hap Wannamaker said.

Sage narrowed his eyes as he regarded his friend.

"I expect there's more to the story. *Did* you find a girl, Yellow Horse?"

Yellow Horse didn't know where to start. So, he just shrugged.

"See, I told you, Cap'n. You owe me a sawbuck. Pay up."

"I'll take it off what you owe me for bailing you out of that faro game in Saltgrass City. And I told you, stop calling me Captain."

"Oh yeah, that. I nearly forgot."

Sage was studying his friend. There was something troubling Yellow Horse. He'd bet on it.

"You boys ride on ahead. I need to palaver with Yellow Horse for a bit. We'll catch up."

When the men were far enough away so they couldn't hear, Sage turned to the scout.

"What's eating at you?"

Yellow Horse scowled.

"Can't you just let it go by, John?"

"I will if you ask me to."

Yellow Horse stared away into the far distance.

Sage waited.

After a time Yellow Horse said, "Her name is Lucy."

Sage waited some more.

"She doesn't belong out here."

Sage nodded his encouragement.

"She is unreasonable and stubborn. I should probably beat her."

Sage held up a hand, shaking his head.

Yellow Horse shrugged.

"It is the way among the Comanche."

"Is she Comanche?"

"No."

Sage waited a moment before he asked, "Did you meet her on the Reservation?"

"You could say that."

Sage rolled his eyes and pulled at his left ear. Yellow Horse could make a sloth lose its patience. By now the departed rangers were just a dust cloud in the distance.

"Is she someone you can talk to?"

"Yes. She's like most white women. She talks too much."

Sage received that bit of news with only a lift of his eyebrows.

"Do you love her?"

"She doesn't belong out here."

"I didn't ask you that."

After a moment, Yellow Horse drew a deep breath and sighed.

"It probably doesn't matter now."

"Why is that?" Sage asked.

"She told me if I wasn't back at Fort Sill in a week, I shouldn't go back at all."

"Uh huh."

"Like a say, it took me three days to find you. I don't know when I'll be able to go back."

"You can go back now, if you want to."

Yellow Horse stared into the distance some more. After a while he took another deep breath and sighed again.

"Let's go see Charlie Goodnight. If this is something you don't need me for, I'll return to Fort Sill." He said.

"What if I do need you?"

"I spent three days looking for you. If you need me, I'm here."

"Lucy might see it differently"

Yellow Horse nodded.

"She does."

Sage leaned on his saddle horn catching his friend's eye.

"I don't want to be the reason you lose the woman you love."

Yellow Horse nodded and looked away. After a while he looked back at Sage. He showed him his shining white teeth in a crooked grin.

He said, "Let's go see Charlie Goodnight, Cap'n Sage."

****

THE END

Authors Note

While this book is a work of fiction, I try to be sensitive to historical accuracy. Although the story is purely a work of my imagination, as is the case with Quanah Parker and Charles Goodnight, many of the other characters who appear in this tale lived in the time and places described.

The history buff might enjoy learning about the life and times of men like, Seldon Lindsey, Captain P.L. Lee and the 10th Cavalry, John Adair, Ben Thompson, James Buchannon Gillett, "Dutch" Henry Bourne, John Reynolds Hughes, Tu-ukumah and Bat Masterson.

It will be understood by the reader that in the process of telling the story, certain liberties were taken with times, events, persons and locations.

Without actually being there, the specific events in the lives of many of these people are the subject of some speculation.

That, as they say, is another story.

***

Thank you for reading **Yellow Horse**.

I would love to hear from you. You can contact me at my website ~ www.danielbanks-books.com or follow me on

YELLOW HORSE

Goodreads ~

https://www.goodreads.com/author/show/10798086.Daniel_Roland_Banks

I hope you had as much fun reading this book as I had writing it. If you liked it please tell a friend - or better yet, tell the world by writing a book review on the book's page on Amazon, or on Goodreads.com.

Even a few short sentences are helpful. As an independently published author, I don't have a marketing department behind me. I only have you, the reader.

So please spread the word!

How do you write a review? It's easy.

Did you like the book? What was your favorite thing about it? Did you learn anything new or interesting? Would you like to read another book by this author?

Go to the Amazon link below, click on the "write a customer review" button and type in your review.

And, to make it a little more fun, if you write a review, e-mail me and I'll return a note, an excerpt from one of my works in progress, maybe even a free e-book.

Thanks again.

All the best,

Dan

DAN ARNOLD

An Excerpt from

BEAR CREEK

Walking over to the livery stable, Clay explained that after he calmed down he realized he'd brought all this on himself. He even thanked me for my offer of help. He also explained that he couldn't stand killing. He hated it, and wouldn't even kill a rattler. He couldn't imagine killing a man.

I was astonished. I asked him why he carried a gun.

"All lawmen do, don't they?"

Clay never ceased to surprise me with his basic honesty and accurate self-assessment. His pride had temporarily blinded him to his responsibility, but it had not goaded him into a fight.

I was all too aware *my* pride had done so. Pride may be the worst sin of all. I apologized for my earlier behavior. I also told him not all lawmen carried guns. There were other options. It could be his choice, either way.

We said hello to Al, then went to the back of the livery where Yellow Horse had his room.

Yellow Horse was standing in the door to his room. Behind him, I could see his things were on the bed, packed and ready to go.

"John," he nodded, "you have my ticket?"

He ignored Clay

"Not yet. Clay would like to say something to you."

Yellow Horse looked at him as if he had just noticed he was there.

Clay looked like he was feeling kind of sick.

"Uh, yeah…you see the thing is…I'm a jackass sometimes…" he trailed off.

Yellow Horse regarded him silently.

"What I mean is…you aren't…uh….." he trailed off again.

Yellow Horse turned to me.

"I will take the train to Denver."

"Yellow Horse, I'm sorry. Really, I acted like an idiot. I shouldn't have said what I said." Clay blurted.

Yellow Horse turned back to face him.

"No?" He raised an eyebrow.

"No, I shouldn't have. I'm sorry I did."

"Yes." Yellow Horse nodded, looking him in the eye.

Clay looked at me, clearly baffled. He had no idea where to go from there.

I did.

"Yes. What?"

Yellow Horse turned to Clay.

"Yes, I accept your apology. Yes, you are an idiot. Yes, if you say it again, I will take your hair."

He turned to me.

"Tell me what you need."

We decided a small party could be prepared and provisioned much more quickly than attempting to put together a larger posse. Even so, by the time we made arrangements and got outfitted for the trip, it was nearly noon.

Clay told us the place where the bank officer was killed was only about a mile above North Fork, but much higher up in the mountains. Because it was pretty much uphill all the way, it would take at least three hours to travel the ten miles to North Fork. Past North Fork the road got narrow and there were many switchbacks. We would need to rest our horses often. It might take nearly another hour to travel the extra mile to the scene of the theft. I wondered if Clay's horse could handle the challenge.

When we rode past Lora's boarding house, she was working in the garden. I stopped to have a word with her, as Yellow Horse and Clay went on.

She and I had been spending some time together. I explained the situation to her, and as I started to remount Dusty, she stopped me and kissed me.

"Be safe out there, and come back to me as soon as you can."

I was more than sufficiently motivated.

I caught up to the others, and as we rode west, I learned the payroll was mostly in gold and silver coins. The miners only got paid once a month and many didn't like paper money. Usually there was about three thousand dollars in coin and paper. To be more secure, the payroll never went up the mountains on the same day of the week. It sometimes went in a strong box on the stage, sometimes on a freight wagon of one kind or another. The freight wagons were frequently on the road, hauling equipment or supplies in, and the ore back out. The stage went to Flapjack City only once a week. The stage was the preferred method of the bank officer who always traveled with the payroll. This time it had been on a freight wagon. This time there had also been more money than usual.

That was a surprise to me.

"Why was that?

"The snow will come soon, so about this time of year they usually send up three or four months' worth of payroll. They secure it up there in the mining offices," Clay said.

"It isn't even fall yet," I pointed out.

"Not down where we live. We have another six weeks or more before it gets frosty, but up there," he pointed toward the top of the mountains, "where the mines are, you can see the old snow. New snow could fly at any time now. They try to keep the roads open, but heavy snows can close the roads for weeks at a time. And there are rock slides and avalanches. It's too dangerous to try to take the payroll up in the winter."

"Your deputies knew that," Yellow Horse observed.

The search party found the body of Preston Lewis slumped in the wagon seat where he had been shot. One deputy had been mounted and one had been driving the team. The deputies and the harness horses were missing. They'd abandoned the buckboard wagon because it was too big to negotiate narrow mountain trails.

It was nearing dusk in the high mountains when we started on their trail. Night comes fast up there, so we wanted to get a sense of where they might be headed. There were few ways they could go, because of the steep mountainsides.

Although the search party had messed up the tracks at the scene of the murder, the thieves trail was obvious from where they left the road. They had headed downhill, along the edge of a narrow creek that ran down into Bear Creek.

Yellow Horse spent some time on foot to become very familiar with the size and shape of the hoof prints their horses were leaving in this soft ground.

"Three men mounted, leading two horses, one is carrying a load." He said.

"That can't be right," Clay said. "There were only two men and they only had three horses."

Yellow Horse shook his head. "Five horses, three men."

"Are you sure about that?"

"I could follow this trail in the dark," Yellow Horse replied.

"That's good, we'll need to. They have a day's start on us," I said.

"We can't keep going in the dark. We'll lose their trail and it's dangerous." Clay opined.

Yellow Horse got back on his mount and continued down the trail. I followed him. The Sheriff of Alta Vista County didn't have much choice, he had to follow us.

We crisscrossed the stream wherever the trail led, letting the horses drink occasionally. We were often moving through chest high thickets of Pussy Willow, working to avoid bogs. Doing that became more important when the sun went down behind the mountains.

At one point we stopped and Yellow Horse got off his horse and studied the ground. He took us up an embankment. We started working our way up the shoulder of a mountain through the spruce and aspen groves, then around and down. It was now fully dark; the only light was that of the moon and stars. The ground here was firm and often rocky. I couldn't see any sign of the trail the thieves had left.

Yellow Horse could.

We had been riding in the dark for hours. We came to an opening in the aspen trees and out into a meadow. The stars above us were spectacular. It was very cold now. I could hear a creek running somewhere.

Dusty pricked his ears forward, something moved at the far edge of the meadow. It could have been an elk, mule deer, or even a moose. It had been that big. Dusty was calm though, and unconcerned. We heard a whinny.

Yellow Horse and I hit the ground holding our reins in one hand and our guns in the other. Clay managed to get down beside us. We waited for a shot that didn't come.

After a minute Yellow Horse motioned he was going to circle around the edge of the meadow. I nodded and took his reins, and he disappeared.

The big thing I had glimpsed materialized at the other edge of the meadow. It was a horse. After a few more minutes we heard a whippoorwill call.

That was the "all clear" signal from Yellow Horse.

I stood up and started out into the meadow, Clay was right behind.

We led our horses across the meadow. Yellow Horse met us part way across.

"We will sleep there," he said, pointing back the way we had come.

"What's wrong with over there?" Clay asked, pointing at the edge of the aspen grove Yellow Horse had just come out of. We could hear the creek just beyond the trees.

"Dead men," Yellow Horse said.

Taking the reins from me, he led his horse past me and I followed him. Clay followed us.

After we had secured our horses and unsaddled them. We gathered together to talk.

"They camped over there," Yellow Horse began, "late last night. They had a picket line for the horses and a small fire. They had food and coffee. Two men were killed, while they slept. There are no horses on the picket line now. I saw two in the meadow grazing. I don't know where the other three horses are or where the third man is. I will look again in daylight."

"OK, let's get some sleep." I directed.

"Wait a minute. Where is the mine payroll, Yellow Horse? Did you see any sign of the money?"

Clay was clearly tired and cranky. We all were.

"John and I will look tomorrow."

"I say we go over there now. We can build a fire and have a look around. At least we can have a hot meal."

"No."

Clay was about to argue some more, but I was too tired to listen to it.

"We'll do it in daylight, Clay. If we stumble around in the dark tonight, we'll just make a mess of any sign that might be over there. Besides, do you really want to sleep over there with the dead bodies?"

"No, I'm just saying…"

"We have maybe four hours till first light. We'll sleep now, if we can." I said.

He didn't like it, but he didn't fight it anymore. We chewed on some jerky and cornbread and drank from our canteens, and then we rolled up in our blankets.

When we woke up, just before sunrise, we had frost on our blankets.

We left our horses tied where they were and walked across the meadow in the gathering daylight.

We found the camp exactly as Yellow Horse had described it. There were two dead men wrapped in blankets, lying beside a new fire ring, made of stones from the creek. Both men had been shot in the head. No animals had been chewing on them, yet.

There was cooking gear and a coffee pot on the edge of the fire ring. I could see a picket line stretched between trees about twenty yards away. We had seen two horses grazing as we crossed the meadow. There was a single pannier, hung high in a tree, over at the edge of the creek. There was also a tarp stretched between trees to form a rain shelter. There were two riding saddles, a pack saddle and some other gear under the tarp.

"I will look around." Yellow Horse said.

I began gathering some of the tinder from the pile of wood at the edge of the fire ring. I started building a fire.

Clay was practically dancing with annoyance and excitement. "What the hell are you doing? We should be looking for the payroll."

"The less we move around right now the better. We'll warm up by the fire and have some coffee. When Yellow Horse gets back, we'll decide how to proceed."

"What about the pannier hanging over there?" He wanted a look in the pack bag that was hanging up in the tree.

"OK, go get it and bring it back here."

He ran over and untied the rope to lower the bag, and then he ran back with it. When he got back he rummaged around in it, but all he found was some bacon, coffee and some canned goods.

"Perfect, we might as well use their supplies." I said, as I lit the fire.

 I handed Clay the coffee pot.

"Take this down to the creek and wash it out, then bring it back, full of water."

"Do you plan to sit here and have breakfast, with these dead men lying here?" He asked.

"No, I plan to sit here and have breakfast with you and Yellow Horse. These boys have lost their appetite. After breakfast, we'll probably carry them back to Bear Creek for burial."

Clay actually stood there with his mouth open.

Yellow Horse came back.

"Are they your deputies?"

He indicated the dead men.

I knew that he already knew the answer, as well as I did.

Clay looked at them a bit more closely. He looked pale and drained.

"Yeah, that's Rogers and the other is Glenn."

"I'll go get our horses and water them at the creek. Are you just going to stand there holding the coffee pot?" Yellow Horse asked Clay.

"What? No…" Clay started.

"Come with me then. You can help with the horses and fill the coffee pot." Yellow Horse turned and Clay walked with him across the meadow.

I took the opportunity to have a quick look around. Close to the tarp, I discovered a place where there was an old, much used campfire ring. Under the tarp there was some stacked firewood. The ground under the tarp was smooth and there was a place where spruce bows had been used to form a mattress. The area around the picket line was trampled and littered with manure. Clearly, the camp had been here for weeks.

I was laying bacon out in a frying pan when Yellow Horse and Clay returned to the fire. As we waited for the coffee to heat, we discussed the situation.

"At the scene of the robbery, there was a man waiting for the wagon, one man alone. He was on foot and probably appeared harmless. He'd secured two saddle horses down by the creek, tied to some willows. I found where they had been tied. He must have been in cahoots with the guards, because they were expecting him. I don't know who killed the bank man. They took the horses and the payroll from the wagon. The three men rode the saddle horses and led the harness horses, one of which was carrying the mine payroll in panniers on a pack saddle. Once they were sure they weren't being followed, they came to this camp, which had been prepared before the robbery," Yellow Horse began.

He looked over at me, to have me take up the narrative.

"They settled in for the night. When it was time for the third man to take the watch, he shot your thieving deputies while they were sleeping."

I looked back to Yellow Horse, who nodded in agreement and said, "The third man turned the horses loose to graze and get water. When he left here in the dark, the other two saddle horses may have followed him. There are many tracks here. It took me awhile to sort it out."

As I put the bacon pan on the coals, Clay asked the obvious question.

"Do you think maybe the third man took the money out, packed on the two harness horses?"

Yellow Horse shook his head.

"No."

"How can you be sure?"

"They are still here."

Yellow Horse pointed to the two horses now grazing close to each other in the meadow."

I could smell the coffee as it began to boil.

"So, maybe he carried it out on the other two saddle horses."

"Maybe," I said "but I don't think so."

"…Why not?" Clay was frustrated and getting impatient.

The bacon began to hiss and sizzle.

I looked back to Yellow Horse, and raised my eyebrows.

He shook his head and said, "He wasn't leading the other two horses. They wandered some. They weren't carrying any kind of load, the saddles and bridles are still here, and so is this pannier."

I took some cold water from a canteen and poured it over the boiling coffee grounds, to settle them.

Clay jumped up.

"Why are we just sitting here? We're burning daylight. We have to track down the third man."

"Yes," I said, as I poured coffee into three cups. "We will. First we have to have breakfast and pack up this camp."

I stirred the bacon some.

"You're crazy; we need to get on the trail now!" Clay shouted.

As the morning sun had begun to drive away the chill, the flies had shown up and began to buzz around the dead men.

I used a fork to pull a piece of bacon out of the pan, gently shaking the extra grease off.

"Clay, settle down. We know what we're doing. We need to eat something, drink some coffee and think for a little bit. Ten minutes won't make a whole lot of difference."

He really didn't have any choice. He was as cold, tired and hungry as we were, and that bacon sure was good. We drank all the coffee and ate all the bacon, using some of our corn bread to sop up the grease.

Sitting by the dead men's fire ring, I gave some thought to what kind of a man would care more about horses, than he did for human beings. The horses had value to him, the people did not.

We often value the wrong things. We can spend our lives working to surround ourselves with things that don't matter. We can sacrifice the things that do matter, to gain those things that don't.

Later, we caught the loose harness horses and packed up what we could. We put the dead men on the pack horses.

We only had that one pannier though.

When we were ready to go, I looked at Yellow Horse, a question in my eyes. He shook his head in response. I shrugged. We mounted up and followed the trail, in the tracks of the killer.

DAN ARNOLD

About the Author

Dan Arnold was born in Bakersfield, California and abandoned by his parents in Seattle, Washington. After living in the foster care system for some years, he was eventually adopted. He's traveled internationally, lived in Idaho, Washington, California, Virginia, and now makes his home in Texas with his wife Lora. They have four grown children of whom they are justifiably proud, not because they are such good parents, but because God is good.

At one (brief) point he was one of the 3% of fine visual artists who earn their entire income from sales of their art. He's a writer, a painter and a sculptor.

In 2013, after 40+ years of searching, he found and got reacquainted with his long lost half-brother and a host of relatives from his mother's side of the family.

A Member of the Association of Christian Fiction Writers, and Western Writers of America, in 2015 his book Angels & Imperfections was selected as a finalist in Christian Fiction in the Reader's Favorite International Book awards.

He is a former Certification and Training Director for CHA, the Association for Horsemanship Safety and Education, former

DAN ARNOLD

Director of the Program for Applied Equine Studies, and a former Master Instructor in both Western and English riding.

As a horse trainer and clinician Dan traveled extensively and was blessed to work with a variety of horses and people in amazing circumstances and locations.

He's herded cattle in Texas, chased kangaroos on horseback through the Australian Outback, guided pack-trips into the Sierras and the Colorado Rockies, conditioned and trained thoroughbred race horses, galloped a warmblood on the bank of a canal that was surveyed by George Washington, and spent uncounted, delightful hours breaking bread with unique characters in diverse parts of the world.

Dan can't sing or dance, but he'd like to think he's considered an accomplished horseman, engaging public speaker, and an excellent judge of single malt Scotch.

Made in the USA
Monee, IL
17 April 2024